Forced into marriage with a much older man after her father catches her in the arms of her female lover, Abigail accepts her lot in life in order to save her family. The love of her life is long gone, cast from her life by her selfless decision, and she must accept that the men in her life—her father and now, her husband—are in control and will do with her as they please.

But after an untimely accident, as her husband lies dying, Abigail realizes there might be a glimmer of hope that she could go free. Will she be strong enough to overcome the obstacles life is putting up and find a way back to the arms of the woman she is yearning for?

A K'Anne Meinel novella

Novels in Paperback:

SHIPS *CompanionSHIP, FriendSHIP,*
RelationSHIP
Long Distance Romance
Children of Another Mother
Erotica
The Claim
Bikini's Are Dangerous
The Complete Series
Germanic
Malice Masterpieces 1
The First Five Books
Represented
Timed Romance
Malice Masterpieces 2
Books Six through Ten
The Journey Home
Out at the Inn
Shorts
Anthology Volume 1
Lawyered
Malice Masterpieces 3
Books Eleven through Fifteen
Blown Away

Blown Away
The Alternate Cover
Small Town Angel
Pirated Love
Doctored
Veil of Silence
Malice Masterpieces 4
Books Sixteen through Twenty
The Outsider
Pirated Heart
Recombinant Love
Survivors
Inn the Dog House
Flight
An Island Between Us

Vetted Series:
Vetted
Cavalcade (Prequel)
Pioneering (Prequel)
Vetted Further
Vetted Again

Novellas in Paperback:

Mysterious Malice (Book 1)
Meticulous Malice (Book 2)
Mistaken Malice (Book 3)
Malicious Malice (Book 4)
Masterful Malice (Book 5)
Matrimonial Malice (Book 6)
Mourning Malice (Book 7)
Murderous Malice (Book 8)
Mental Malice (Book 9)
Menacing Malice (Book 10)
Minor Malice (Book 11)
Morally Malice (Book 12)
Morose Malice (Book 13)
Melancholy Malice (Book 14)
Mad Malice (Book 15)
Macabre Malice (Book 16)
Marinating Malice (Book 17)

Macerating Malice (Book 18)
Minacious Malice (Book 19)
Meddlesome Malice (Book 20)
Meandering Malice (Book 21)
Vaquera Safica (Spanish)
Surfista Safica (Spanish)
ケーアンヌ・マイネル (Japanese)
Maniacal Malice (Book 22)
Sayyida
The Northwood Lodge
Monitoring Malice (Book 23)
Marked Malice (Book 24)
Shanghaied
Outback Born
Outback Bred
Outback Heritage

Pocket Paperbacks:

Mysterious Malice (Book 1)
Sapphic Surfer
Sapphic Cowgirl
Meticulous Malice (Book 2)
Mistaken Malice (Book 3)
Malicious Malice (Book 4)
Masterful Malice (Book 5)
Matrimonial Malice (Book 6)
Mourning Malice (Book 7)
Murderous Malice (Book 8)

Mental Malice (Book 9)
Menacing Malice (Book 10)
Minor Malice (Book 11)
Morally Malice (Book 12)
Morose Malice (Book 13)
Melancholy Malice (Book 14)
Mad Malice (Book 15)
Macabre Malice (Book 16)
Marinating Malice (Book 17)

In E-Book Format:
Short Stories

Fantasy
Wet & Wet Again
Family Night
Quickie ~ Against the Car
Quickie ~ Against the Wall
Quickie ~ Over the Couch
Mile High Club
Quickie ~ Under the Pier
Heel or Heal
Kiss
Family Night 2
Beach Dreams
Internet Dreamers
Snoggered

On the Parkway
Stable Affair
Kept
Stolen
Agitated
Love of my LIFE
Quickie in an Elevator,
GOING DOWN?
Into the Garden
The Book Case
The Other Women
Menage a WHAT?

E-Book Novellas

Children of Another Mother
Bikini's are Dangerous
Ghostly Love
Bikini's are Dangerous 2
Sapphic Surfer
The Rockhound
Bikini's are Dangerous 3
Bikini's are Dangerous 4
Bikini's are Dangerous 5
Mysterious Malice (Book 1)
Meticulous Malice (Book 2)
Mistaken Malice (Book 3)
Malicious Malice (Book 4)
Masterful Malice (Book 5)
Matrimonial Malice (Book 6)
Mourning Malice (Book 7)
Murderous Malice (Book 8)
Sapphic Cowgirl
Sapphic Cowboi
Mental Malice (Book 9)
Menacing Malice (Book 10)
Charming Thief
~Snake Island~

Charming Thief
~Diamonds are a Girls Best Friend~
Minor Malice (Book 11)
Morally Malice (Book 12)
Morose Malice (Book 13)
Melancholy Malice (Book 14)
Mad Malice (Book 15)
Macabre Malice (Book 16)
Marinating Malice (Book 17)
Macerating Malice (Book 18)
Minacious Malice (Book 19)
Sayyida
Meddlesome Malice (Book 20)
Meandering Malice (Book 21)
Maniacal Malice (Book 22)
The Northwood Lodge
Monitoring Malice (Book 23)
Marked Malice (Book 24)
Shanghaied
Outback Born
Outback Bred
Outback Heritage

E-Book Novels

SHIPS *CompanionSHIP, FriendSHIP, RelationSHIP*
Erotica Volume 1
Long Distance Romance
Bikini's Are Dangerous
The Complete Series
Malice Masterpieces
The First Five Books
To Love a Shooting Star
Germanic
The Claim
Represented
Timed Romance
Blown Away
Blown Away *The Alternate Cover*
Malice Masterpieces 2
Books Six through Ten
The Journey Home
Out at the Inn
Anthology Volume 1
Lawyered

Malice Masterpieces 3
Books Eleven through Fifteen
Small Town Angel
Pirated Love
Doctored
Veil of Silence
Malice Masterpieces 4
Books Sixteen through Twenty
The Outsider
Pirated Heart
Recombinant Love
Survivors
Inn the Dog House
Flight
An Island Between Us

Vetted Series:
Vetted
Cavalcade (Prequel)
Pioneering (Prequel)
Vetted Further
Vetted Again

LARGE Print Novels

SHIPS CompanionSHIP, FriendSHIP, RelationSHIP
Erotica Volume 1
Long Distance Romance
Children of Another Mother
Bikini's Are Dangerous
The Complete Series

Malice Masterpieces
The First Five Books
To Love a Shooting Star
The Claim
Represented
Timed Romance

Audiobooks

Cavalcade
Doctored
Flight
Ghostly Love
Love of My Life
Mysterious Malice
Meticulous Malice
Pioneering

Sapphic Cowgirl
Sapphic Surfer
Sayyida
Stable Affair
The Rockhound
The Bookcase
To Love A Shooting Star
Vetted

K'ANNE MEINEL

OUTBACK YEARNINGS

ISBN-13: 978-1733661171

K'Anne Meinel is available for comments at KAnneMeinel@aim.com as well as on Facebook @ http://www.facebook.com/K.Anne.Meinel.Fan.Page, Google + @ https://plus.google.com/u/2/+KAnneMeinel, LinkedIn @ https://www.linkedin.com/in/k-anne-meinel-a026385a, or her blog @ http://kannemeinel.wordpress.com/ or on Twitter @ https://twitter.com/KAnneMeinel, or on her website @ www.kannemeinel.com if you would like to follow her to find out about stories and book's releases.

www.shadoepublishing.com

ShadoePublishing@gmail.com

Shadoe Publishing, LLC is a United States of America company

Cover by: K'Anne Meinel @ Shadoe Publishing
Edited by: Deb Amia, Grammar Queen grammarqueen.com

**Dedicated to anyone who
thinks I'm writing about them.
I am.**

CHAPTER ONE

Lady Abigail Baxter Worthington, Countess Worthington, stared out the long Gothic windows of the Worthington Estate, which was named Hedgerows for the many beautiful mazes and sculpted figurines about the estate. They had an army of gardeners who kept it trimmed and impeccably beautiful. It was raining, and the water spattered against the double windows in this section of the room that was repeated over and over along the walls. The gray of the day reflected her mood as she watched the sheets of water coming down. She heard a creak upstairs, probably from her husband's rooms and prayed, not that he would live but that he would die. He needed to be out of the pain she had watched him suffer for weeks now, ever since he had been kicked by one of their horses and the resulting hematoma had spread instead of healing. Ultimately, it had caused a fit of sorts…a stroke.

The doctors had bled him, further weakening him and making it difficult for him to heal. He had called his wife to his bed just that morning to talk to her.

"Well, my dear, it is time," he told her, his voice sounding raspy and weak, almost a whistle in its reedy tenor.

"No, not yet," she pleaded with him, looking scared. She wasn't merely scared, she was terrified. During the years of their marriage, he had proven to be her ally, her defense against her father's irritation over this forced marriage. Lord Worthington had kept her father from bullying her. He had protected her from her father's anger, blackmail, and his incessant need for monies. She had cheered when Augustus had told him, "No more!" and cut off Lord Baxter and his bottomless pockets.

Lord Baxter had married his oldest daughter to the earl, not only to hide the family's shame brought on by the American woman who had seduced his daughter, but also to deal with the fact that Lord Baxter was seriously in debt and on the verge of a very embarrassing bankruptcy brought on by his incessant gambling. Once his initial debts were paid off on the marriage of Abigail to Lord Worthington, he had thought to capitalize on the relationship. Certain his luck had changed; he began betting even more beyond his means and was racking up further debt. He was astonished when Worthington had finally refused to provide any more help in the form of loans he would never repay. He would have been astounded to learn that his daughter, who hadn't wanted to marry the old earl in the first place, had pleaded with her husband to cut her father off.

"I can well afford your father's debts," he had told her reasonably, amused when she asked him to stop making her father these incessant loans.

"Don't you see? He will never stop," she answered, embarrassed on her father's behalf. Lord Baxter couldn't see that the well might someday run dry. He owned several properties that he had borrowed heavily against, and if not for his daughter's marriage, he would have lost them all by now. He also had her brothers and little sister to think of, but he did not. Her marriage had netted him a fortune, and he seemed determined to run through that as quickly as he had his own.

Lord Worthington had finally acceded to his wife's wishes, giving Lord Baxter an ultimatum. The Lord, a lesser earl, finally realized that Worthington was not going to give him any further loans. For a time, he curbed his gambling. But a sickness had developed, and he couldn't help himself. He started with small bets again, and then, when he was winning, he bet larger and larger amounts. For a time, he was very successful, but as was the case with many gamblers, he didn't know when to stop. He was still ahead but knew this could not last. His oldest son was now married and expecting an heir, and they were planning for his youngest daughter's wedding, and she was marrying quite well. Lost in his own delusions, he was certain not only that his luck had changed, but either his son's marriage, or his other daughter's marriage would bring him ready capital.

Hearing that the Earl of Worthington was sickly, he began to plot how he could obtain his oldest daughter's wealth. After all, as her oldest, living, male relative, he would be able to administer her wealth for her. No court would deny him as her father. Perhaps, he could eventually marry her off again, this time to an even wealthier man. She was still young enough to provide another man with heirs; she had given the older earl a daughter.

"Do you think this one will be a son?" the old earl asked his wife, smiling at her rounding figure that was hidden so well in the dress she wore. He had chosen the fabric and the design, and expensive materials and a skillful seamstress had been hired to create Lady Worthington's wardrobe as Augustus approved it. The styles were old-fashioned and suited his tastes, not the young woman's. They were reminiscent of what his mother had worn, but she knew better than to object.

Abigail smoothed her hand down her figure, revealing the faint bulge that signified she was pregnant again. She smiled at her elderly husband, fond of the man who had understood her young girl's fears and brought her to their marriage bed so gently. He had never spoken of the reason for their rather hasty marriage or the woman she had been caught with. She didn't know that he had dismissed it as a youthful indiscretion and felt it didn't count since it was with a woman. Her maidenhead was intact, which he had discovered when she had been able to arouse him enough that he could battle against it. He felt certain that the daughter she had given him precisely ten months after the date of their marriage was his, and he was also certain that this child she was carrying would be the longed-for heir. He had realized when marrying the eighteen-year-old Abigail Baxter that he had left it far too long to have an heir. At fifty-eight, he worried he would be unable to sire a child on her young body, but she had inspired him, and he'd been able to service her regularly, at least once a week, until she conceived.

"No, no my dear. Do not move," he had instructed her when Abigail attempted to simulate some sort of passion between her and her husband. "I don't want you acting the harlot." He had instructed her on their marriage night that he would visit her weekly. She was to remain modest and in her gown but to wear no underclothes. She was not to look at him and simply submit to his masculine desire. "I know what we do is for procreation, but the sin of it…" he lamented as he puffed over her, playing with her breasts to get himself aroused and thrusting into her before he could lose his erratic and sometimes errant erection.

Abigail had lain there, humiliated, as the old man played with her body, wishing her husband was younger, more vibrant or virile, or that it was Melissa Lawrence there instead. She could arouse herself with thoughts of Melissa, but her husband discouraged arousal, wanting her to lay there and take his seed like the good wife she was to become. He instructed her in every way, taking charge of her life, and Abigail obeyed. Her spirit was broken by depression, heartbreak, and the marriage her father had contracted for her.

Melissa Lawrence was gone from her life, gone to London or so the gossip said. Melissa's father had passed away, and while Abigail had wanted to go to the funeral, she knew she wouldn't be allowed. She had written a letter to Melissa, not intending to send it, but when she learned that Melissa had gone back to New York, she finally had an address for the woman and sent it on. She learned that Melissa, who was now going by Mel, had moved on from New York to Virginia and the farm she owned there, then on to New Orleans. She only heard from her sporadically as she became a cowboy and was working on several ranches in the west. Imagine that, an American cowboy! Then she had gone on to own her own herd and was taking them to starving miners in California. Abigail hadn't heard from her again for a while and thought perhaps, her husband or his staff were keeping her correspondence from her, and then one day, she received a letter from Sydney, Australia! It had surprised her to learn that Mel intended to stay there, start over, and find something that she would enjoy.

Abigail had felt quite sorry for herself. Her days were rather boring, and the books in her husband's library were minimal and ancient. Her husband had a competent housekeeper, who made it very clear that an eighteen-year-old girl would not be taking over the household she had managed for over twenty-five years. Although Abigail felt there was a lot she could learn from the woman, any knowledge was grudgingly imparted. Mrs. Leister had many good years left and would not be giving up her position to this mere slip of a girl. Her attitude transcended to the rest of the staff as the cook, the butler, and even the maids tended to take their cue from this formidable woman. They didn't dare cross the powerful housekeeper for this young girl, and Abigail, depressed and thoroughly intimidated by the woman, didn't take them in hand. As a result, they walked all over the new lady of the house.

Still, it wasn't all bad. Augustus was kind to her in his own way, but he did feel that he owned her, and everything she had was due to him. Fortunately, Abigail had realized this too and catered to him and his ego, for her and her family's sake. Her mother could visit, and her sister was excited about her new position. Lady Worthington far outclassed the Baxter family now, the social status of the Worthingtons being much higher than that of the Baxters. Because of her marriage and status, Robert, her elder brother and the Baxter heir, had contracted a better marriage, greatly enhancing the Baxter name. Her other brother, Anthony—named for their father and the one who had tried to woo Melissa Lawrence—had gone off on adventures to seek his own fortune. As the second born son of a slightly impoverished earl, he was not the catch he had hoped he was. Finding out that Melissa was attracted to his sister, he had jumped on the family band wagon and admonished his sister for her unconscionable actions. She hadn't seen him since her marriage to the earl and didn't care to. Her little sister had contracted a marriage to another earl, a peer of her husband's, who, while not nearly as old, was still in his late thirties, almost forty. Lady Baxter had implored her eldest daughter to help her younger sister by using her household monies to help dress the girl and provide a trousseau befitting a girl of her now elevated station. Abigail didn't mind, and Augustus hadn't either when she asked his permission.

The only real enjoyment Abigail had was going down to the stables, which were situated a considerable distance from their enormous mansion in order to keep the smells well away from them. The stables at the home farm encompassed enormous pastures and many acres of lush land where the animals were bred, raised, ridden, and trained. It was a beautiful setup, one of several that the earl owned. She loved walking down here and riding. She was always dressed in the proper riding attire as per her husband's edict, and always rode sidesaddle, as he thought a lady should. Many times, she found herself riding out with her grooms following her, and she would end up just sitting on a hill overlooking the lush farmlands of her husband's estate. She enjoyed the view. It was beautiful, but it wasn't home to her, and she missed her mother. She'd stare out at the lands, watching farmers tilling their fields, animals in the other fields, and birds flying in the beautiful skies, and she would wonder what Melissa Lawrence was doing and what her life was like now. She wondered what Australia

was like. No one knew much about it other than it had been a penal colony, and she wondered how the American was faring there. All she could do was wait and hope she would get another letter.

Her enjoyment of her riding was curtailed when she found herself pregnant, and getting pregnant so soon after their wedding, she had had such a limited time on horseback. After Agatha was born, she couldn't ride for a while as the doctor told Augustus she shouldn't. It took a long while for her to get pregnant again, and her escape was in these rides. She enjoyed the many wonderful horses she had at her disposal during this time.

Still, on days like this, Abigail wondered if her life was worthwhile. She wasn't welcome in her own home, although Augustus wouldn't have seen it that way. He felt she was a perfect little wife for him. She didn't have any of the traits her father had warned him about. She deferred to him on every decision, and she obeyed him in everything. Occasionally, when they had an actual conversation, he enjoyed that she could talk intelligently about horses. He loved the stables and farms he had acquired when that American upstart had died, and his daughter had sold most of his equine assets. He felt he had gotten a bargain, not aware that Melissa had sold it all for a substantial profit. He hadn't dealt with her, instead, dealing with the male solicitors who represented her. He hadn't realized that the American's daughter was equally savvy and had instructed these men on the exact prices she wanted for the land, the buildings, and the amazing animals her father had purchased. The extraordinary idea that a woman, any woman, could be astute at business had never entered the earl's mind.

CHAPTER TWO

The Earl of Worthington had obtained his massive wealth through the mills his father and older brother had invested in, building up towns where the increasing sheep's wool industry in England and eventually the colonies was carded and turned into cloth to be sold all over the world. These massive mills had continued to grow and were now huge complexes owned by a handful of men from all over Britain. Upon the earl's older brothers' untimely death, Augustus had become the heir to the title Earl of Worthington. He was someone who hadn't wanted to run the mills, just obtain more of them, and Augustus, who had worked in the mills to learn them from the ground up, had eventually taken them over. Upon his father's death, he had trained men to run them for him, so he could indulge in more of life's pleasures, namely, raising horses, which he loved.

Horse racing was a huge spectator sport in Britain. It was one of the longest established sports with a history that went back many centuries to Roman times. Many of the rules even originated in those times. He was proud when horses from his stables competed on the racecourses of Newmarket, Ascot, and Cheltenham, then later competed in the iconic races that included The Derby at Epsom, The Grand National, and the Cheltenham Gold Cup. He employed some of the best jockeys in racing and paid them only a little better than some of his competitors, so he could keep them.

Lord Worthington's stables produced some of the best Thoroughbreds in the world, and with the addition of the mares and stallions that the American had acquired from England and Europe, he was certain they were now the best. The names entered in the General Stud Book, first published by James Weatherby back in the 17th and 18th centuries, were prime stock.

Lord Worthington occasionally bet on the races and always on his own horses, but he rarely lost vast sums of money like the beleaguered Lord Baxter, who bet on a whim. Lord Baxter didn't thoroughly research the horses, and as a result, he lost almost as often as he won. Lord Worthington had many times the capital to lose than Baxter and rarely lost.

Finding out that Lord Baxter was in dire straits, he made an offer for the pretty, young Lady Baxter. Her purple eyes entranced him, and he thought she would breed up fine sons for him. She appeared healthy, and her dam had bred up fine sons and daughters for her husband from what he could see, so he never thought Abigail would do otherwise for himself. The fact that he was nearly impotent didn't enter the old earl's mind. He was still able to get it up occasionally, and his wife would submit to his carnal side at his leisure. He thought he had years to breed up a healthy brood of heirs. He was disappointed that the first child they produced was a girl. It had never occurred to him that she wouldn't give him a son; After all, he *wanted* a son. The girl child was interesting, but she wasn't the desired male heir, so they would have to try again. Abigail was a good girl, despite having given him a girl child when he wanted a boy, and she submitted obligingly to his needs. In another time, Lord Worthington, a second son, would have been an excellent candidate for the priesthood; however, there would have then been no Worthington estate to leave to his heir as it would have all gone to the church. Now, since he had a wife and daughter and the possibility of a son and heir, Lord Worthington arrogantly assumed he would live forever. He was wrong.

The fit that struck him down after the horse kicked him and left him bed ridden came upon him suddenly. He was brought back from one of the outlying farms on a stretcher that seemed to exacerbate his condition. He lay in agony as the doctors fussed over his supine body, his young wife kept out in the hall where the servants came and went, anxiously awaiting news. The doctors were incompetent, and despite their bloodletting procedure, which made him weaker, he was only getting worse.

"Abigail my darling girl, come sit here beside me," he rasped when she was allowed in to see her husband by the doctors. They admonished her not to 'tire' the earl, and she was annoyed by their attitudes. They had tired him considerably with their endless tests attempting to heal him from his condition. That he was now dying was obvious to anyone who saw him.

The man had been kind to her, so she could afford to be a good wife to him. *"Oh, Augustus,"* she cried, running to his side, taking his outstretched hand in hers, and putting it to her cheek.

"Now, now, my dear, you must listen to me. I do not have much time, and these fools," he gestured to the doctors who had left the chamber and wouldn't have appreciated his assessment of their skills, "have drained me. I'm dying."

Abigail would have to agree with him. He looked horrible. With the curtains closed and in the muted light of the candles he looked like a cadaver in the folds of his blankets, the shadows making his bones stick out prominently on his elderly face.

"I hadn't yet changed my will for our son," he rasped, indicating her stomach. No one knew of the impending heir. "You will have to manage for him until he is old enough to take the reins of responsibility," he instructed her as he had on many things in the three years since their marriage. "My solicitors will make sure you are taken care of," he rasped out, sure that the men he had dealt with over the years could handle this young woman. After all, how could a mere child, *a woman*, handle his vast estates. It was unthinkable.

She bowed her head subserviently but something about the verbiage he always used made her want to rebel. She hid that side of herself, ever the obedient wife. She simply nodded.

He smiled to himself. She was well trained and had served him well. He would have liked to watch half a dozen heirs grow. Even girl children were useful for arranging marriages to men he would like to align his pedigree with. He could have had one son for an heir, another for the church, and another for the army, if he had only had the *time*. He cursed the fates for not allowing him to find this kind of girl sooner.

He'd been so wrapped up in amassing his wealth, he had missed out on several opportunities to start sooner. "Now, be a good girl and obey my solicitors. They know best," he told her condescendingly from where they were holding them together on his bed as he patted her hand. "Let me sleep," he ordered.

Nodding again, Abigail kissed the back of his hand as she thought a good wife should do. Straightening the bed clothes and then tucking him in, she left him in peace and quiet and went out into the hall where the doctors were conversing. "You may stay in our sitting room," she indicated the room that separated the two master bedrooms. She had rarely been in her husband's room; he had always come to hers. "I'll have refreshments brought for you while you keep your watch," she told them politely, avoiding their eyes, her beautiful violet-colored eyes downcast in her sorrow over the situation.

Now, she watched the rain out the window, wondering what she would do next. Agatha, her daughter—God, how she detested that name, but Augustus had insisted, saying it was his maternal mother's name and part of his Prussian origins—was being taken care of by her governess. The woman had been recommended by Mrs. Leister and was of the same ilk. Abigail knew she didn't like the woman, and the feeling was mutual. The woman didn't think this young girl knew anything about mothering, and she let it show. Abigail caressed her rounding belly, pleased that only her husband knew. She wondered if the laundress had reported to the housekeeper yet. She obviously hadn't had her time of the month since no rags had been in the laundry. Once that news was out to the staff, there would be no keeping it a secret; news like that would spread among their tenants and out to their friends, and she hated that. She had no friends in this household. The

friends she'd had before her marriage, few, if any, were on the same social standing as she and were intimidated by her elderly husband. If her husband didn't scare them off, her staff did with their snooty ways. She knew they had turned away one or two because they had told her when they saw them at some event. Her only escape had been her husband's excellent stables, which was one of the few things they'd had in common for the last three years, but he didn't listen to her as had Mr. Lawrence, Melissa's father. He was condescendingly superior to her, his grooms taking their cue from him, and even the stable boys gave her looks that said she was merely a woman and couldn't possibly know anything about the horses. It had been her idea to purchase the various stables that Melissa Lawrence was selling when her father died, but that was forgotten as the lineage of these horses was recorded and discussed and plans were made for their care and breeding.

Abigail wondered what she would do once her husband passed. She looked around the fine estate she and her husband lived in, feeling the ghosts of his ancestors about her. She rubbed her arms, always feeling cold in this mausoleum. It was like a huge tomb and not the warm mansion it could be. When she asked for more wood in her bedroom or in the living room where she was expected to sew or do needlepoint all day long, it was grudgingly brought to her, or Mrs. Leister came to assess if she really needed the wood. Frequently, she was denied the privilege of extra wood to burn. The woman went so far as to suggest that she put on a sweater or a wrap. It was all so frustrating.

"Lady Worthington?" the butler interrupted her musings.

Abigail looked up, hearing the note of sorrow in the man's voice. She knew the servants adored Lord Worthington. They'd all been with him a long time and were completely loyal to the man even if they

thought his choice in brides to be a twit. She'd heard them use that very word and while hurt, she was aware she had no allies in this house. "Yes, Mr. Franklin?" she returned, hoping she sounded authoritative like the snooty butler.

"It is time, madam," he said, and she couldn't help but notice he sounded disapproving. She wasn't sure if it was her or the situation he disapproved of but chose not to think too deeply about it.

Abigail sighed, unable to think of anything else but Augustus' passing. She went to sit with her husband, heard his labored breathing, and realized the doctors were not leaving his bedroom this time. They wanted to be sure they were there when the old earl passed in order to attest to his death and assure each other they had done all they could for the important man. Abigail sat there, leaning in and holding the hand. It was like holding sandpaper. He hadn't been washed in days, and there was an odor emanating from his emaciated body; there was an odor of death in the air. She would have liked to open the windows and bring in fresh air for him to breathe, but the rain, the cold, and their shocked countenance would prevent her from doing anything like that. She sat there and waited and thought about what had led up to her becoming this elderly man's bride.

CHAPTER THREE

Abigail remembered meeting Melissa Lawrence when her father and she came up for the races. That day had been raining too, and it delayed the race they were watching. Seeing the large woman, she studied her and impulsively stated, "Oh, that outfit is divine. Did you have it made in London?"

Melissa had looked down at Abigail, and the young girl knew what the older woman saw. Abigail was blonde, petite, and had lovely purple eyes. Melissa was wearing a stylish riding habit. She smiled at the younger girl and shook her head. "No, I had it made in New York City."

"Oh, you're from the colonies," she said, clapping her hands together in delight at having discovered this and Mel's accent giving her away.

Mel smiled at the reference. America hadn't been a colony in quite some time. "Yes, I am."

"Do you ride there?"

"I do try. I enjoy a nice horse."

"Do you ride astride," she lowered her voice at that word, "or sidesaddle?"

"I've ridden both," she admitted, wondering at this young woman so full of questions. She was a pretty little thing, and her eyes shone in her delight.

"Isn't it decadent to ride astride?" she asked, keeping her voice lowered as she glanced about, hoping no one would hear the indelicate conversation.

"It's more comfortable," Mel admitted. She looked up in time to see her father coming over.

"Melissa, I've managed to commit myself to the race for Sir McKenzie," he told her, rolling his eyes but grinning delightedly.

"Father don't tell me you didn't finagle that invitation," she admonished, shaking a finger at him in mock outrage.

"Well, I did imply that I wanted to see how good his offspring were," he said as he patted the horse he was leading.

"That is Grover. He is a bit of a dud," Abigail told him knowledgeably.

"And you are?" he asked, surprised at the young woman and her unsolicited opinion.

"I am sorry. We haven't been properly introduced," the young woman said, holding her hand up to her mouth in shock at her manners as she glanced between Mel and her father.

"I am Melissa Lawrence, and this is my father, Victor Lawrence," Mel quickly amended. "Since no one else is about to introduce us, this will have to do."

The woman nodded before curtsying prettily to Melissa's father. "Mr. Lawrence, Miss Lawrence, I am Abigail Baxter."

"Miss Baxter." Victor Lawrence doffed his hat to the young girl, wondering how his daughter had met this pretty little piece of baggage.

"Lady Baxter," she corrected automatically, and her hand went to her mouth again in surprise at her audacity.

"Lady Baxter," he repeated dutifully, never fully understanding the complexities of the European aristocracy. Not too many of them were in business, finding it beneath them and instead, depending on rents and inherited wealth to sustain their lifestyles. Few understood that eventually that would all change, and to sustain their livelihoods they would have to diversify into such common pursuits as business. "And how do you know of this horse?" He indicated the horse he was leading.

"Sir McKenzie bred his mare to a truly bad stallion," she said, lowering her voice again as she shared the information. "Ask him to let you ride Roy-Boy. Now, there is a ride I'm certain you will enjoy."

Victor Lawrence studied the girl, smiling and wondering how she knew horses so well. He thought, perhaps, she was as astute as his own daughter, and with a nod, he led the horse away to seek Sir McKenzie. He knew it wouldn't be beyond the gentleman's odd English sense of humor to put him on a dud. He would ask for Roy-Boy, the horse the girl had recommended.

"Are you really a lady?" Mel asked with an impish grin.

Abigail nodded. "Are you really an American?" she teased in return. It was the first time in a long time that Mel had seen the tentative beginnings of a friendship, and she was delighted it was with so pretty a gal. She returned the young woman's grin; unaware this was the beginning of a friendship that would change both their lives.

Abigail returned to the present, looking at the old man dying before her and hearing the murmurings of her husband's inept doctors. She knew she should have sent for a younger doctor, but she also knew that wouldn't have been allowed. Any commands she might have made to the staff would have been ignored. As she thought about that situation, she became angry. She was the lady of this house and should be obeyed. Then she glanced at her dying husband and realized he wouldn't have *allowed* it. It was his home, and she was a mere chattel.

Abigail allowed herself to dwell on her memories for a moment again. They were the only things she had had for years in her dismal existence.

Mel had been a delight. She hadn't understood the various lords and ladies of the realm, and try as she might, Abigail couldn't seem to help it make sense to the American. It was amusing and exasperating at the same time. Her friends couldn't understand her new friendship with the woman who looked a bit frumpy in the dresses she wore. Her clothes were made of all the best materials but nothing could make the big woman look feminine.

"No, no, no," she tried to explain that her family, the Baxters, were part of the Earl of Pembleton's extended family. "It means our family are accorded privileges others would not be."

"Just because you are related?" Mel had been surprised. "Not for anything you have done or anything your father has accomplished?"

"Well, my father…" she began ashamedly, but as her friendship with Mel had deepened, she confided that he enjoyed the horses but especially loved to gamble. His countenance was off-putting. He was an enormously fat man and not especially well educated, despite having attended some of England's best schools.

Melissa Lawrence's father seemed to be a self-made man, something that was fascinating to the Englishwoman. No one she had ever met was self-made. His decision to invest in beautiful Thoroughbreds in England appealed to the young woman. It was fascinating to see the Americans and hear their stories. He had been purchasing horses throughout England but was now looking into investing in a Thoroughbred farm.

"It can be traced back to the three foundation sires imported to England in the early eighteenth century," Melissa told her, proud of her father.

Abigail had news of her own as they watched another race. "Daddy lost again," she confided, worried as she watched her father drink away his bitterness.

Mel wasn't sure what to say to her new friend, afraid it would come out wrong. She adroitly changed the conversation back to the Thoroughbreds they were watching. She found Abigail a fountain of information where they were concerned.

"James Weatherby recorded the details of every horse in the breed," Abigail had advised Mr. Lawrence, and it was with this young girl's knowledge, which continually surprised the man, that he considered his purchases.

"What will you do?" Mel finally ventured to ask, feeling odd that they were discussing her friend's family finances.

"Oh, he'll win it back," she said airily, her hand dismissing the money as though it meant nothing.

Mel wasn't so sure of that. She had bet from time to time, more as a diversion but knowing if she lost the money it was for amusement only, not for the purpose of getting ahead with the funds she was certain she would win. She had met Sir Baxter, a man she was certain shouldn't drink or gamble but who couldn't seem to help himself. She also met Lady Baxter, a petite woman, who was pleased with her daughter's American friend. Abigail's brothers were tolerant of the older woman who had befriended their little sister, and Abigail's younger sister didn't seem to notice anything but the puppies in the stable. Mel was fascinated by this big family. She knew her own mother and father had intended to have more children, and she often wished she had siblings, but remembering some of the women her father had considered as possible mates, perhaps not.

Mel had been surprised when Abigail's second-born brother, Anthony, had taken an interest in her. Suspicious that it was her father's money and not her person that appealed to him, she kept him on a friendship level. Not used to having women who only wanted to be friends with him, he was confused.

"Tony wants to be your beau," Abigail teased. She knew of her brother's interest, having heard it being discussed at the dinner table.

"I'm not interested," Mel admitted sincerely. She knew she wasn't attractive to men in general, and the few who had showed a genuine interest were too late, in her opinion. She now knew where her inclinations lay. She looked at Abigail, wondering, not for the first time, if she could ever confide in her friend. She would probably shock the seventeen-year-old girl. She looked at the other friends she had made, none of them as close to her as Abigail Baxter, and she knew she could never confide in them either. They wouldn't understand.

"Why not? He won't be the earl like Robert, but he is still related to earls and will have the second son's portion." Abigail sounded genuinely curious.

"Don't you want to love your partner?"

"My partner?" she asked, surprised by the word the American used.

"Your husband?" she amended, realizing she had to be careful. The young woman wasn't as worldly as Mel felt she was.

"Well, that's not always possible in our world," she said practically, and Mel was shocked. She knew that they married for status, but she hadn't thought they would completely dismiss all thoughts of love.

"Everyone deserves love," Mel answered, sounding almost sad as she wondered if she would ever have it. She knew her father loved her, even Edith had loved her when they were in New York, but she wasn't sure she would ever experience the love between two spouses.

"Of course, they do, silly. My children will know I love them. There are those," she lowered her voice, so they wouldn't be overheard as she explained, "who take a lover after they have given their husband heirs." She sounded intrigued. Now, as she looked at her husband dying, she wondered if she would ever have had the opportunity to take a lover. She caressed her stomach, the baby inside was so small, barely noticeable, and she knew her husband probably wouldn't have visited her bed again if this were a boy and he had an heir. He had once, in a moment of frivolity, mentioned he wanted many children from her, but she knew now that would never happen.

"That's frowned upon," Mel had pointed out, trying not to laugh at the young woman's romantic notions of what love could be.

Apparently, it wasn't associated with a husband that was chosen more for his status and situation than for anything romantic.

"Of course, it's the forbidden part that is the most appealing!"

Mel enjoyed the spark she saw in her friend's young eyes. They ran into each other time and time again as her father negotiated for his investments in the Thoroughbreds and arranged for someone to manage them for him since he wouldn't be directly overseeing the farms or the horses. His money would be put up and someone else would get the acclaim, but ultimately, the profits, if any, would be his.

"What do you see in that American? She's so...so provincial," Abigail's other friends asked her, sounding snooty and condescending.

"She's a delight! She's like a breath of fresh air, and I don't find her provincial in the least," she faithfully defended her newest friend, sure her friends were just jealous.

"Look, there is the Earl of Worthington," Abigail pointed out one day as they all met at a race. She saw that Mel was dressed tastefully in a gown that didn't really flatter her dark good looks but at least was stylish. Her friends had noted, cattily she thought, that Mel wasn't competition for any of their beaus. No one with a title would marry an *American*. They were wrong but young enough to think they knew it all.

"And who is he?" Mel asked, unable to keep up with the many earls, lords, and ladies she had met in her father's travels. Once, she had even met a duke, which she understood was another name for a prince. She relied on this friend of hers to help her keep them straight.

"He's an enormously successful breeder of Thoroughbreds. He is the *Earl of Worthington*," she finished, as though that should mean something to Mel. At her puzzled and uncomprehending look, Abigail went on to explain that he was very wealthy, had never married, and at the age of fifty-four many wondered if he intended to let his line die out along with his noble title. "I've heard he prefers young men," she confided in a whisper, much to Mel's shock. Mel was surprised she would know such a thing and wondered if the naive blonde understood what that meant. "He also owns mills and other manufactories."

"I'm sure my father would wish to make his acquaint–" Mel had started to say when Abigail put her hand on her friend's arm to stop her. She nodded towards the two men, who were animatedly speaking, having obviously made each other's acquaintance already.

Abigail had been astounded to receive an invitation, tendered to her father, to go to Belgium with the Lawrences. Victor was going on a buying trip and taking Melissa, and he thought Melissa might enjoy the company of her friend. He liked the young girl; He thought she was a good influence on his daughter and really appreciated how much the girl knew about horses. It had been young Abigail's advice that had led to his purchase of the horse farm. She knew things about the breed as well as those in the industry he was investing so heavily in.

Lord and Lady Baxter agreed to allow Abigail to accompany her American friend and her father but only if he further agreed to a chaperone for the young girl. Melissa was far too young to chaperone their precious older daughter, and if they were to allow her to go, someone must be found. Upon hearing her parents' requirement for a chaperone, Abigail put forth the name of her old nanny. Mrs. Jessup, who always enjoyed traveling, agreed to chaperone the impressionable young woman on their trip to Belgium with the American's father.

"This is going to be so much fun," Abigail said delightedly, squeezing Melissa's arm in excitement as they sailed across the English Channel to Belgium.

Mel's father had made all the arrangements, pleased to give the girls such a treat. Mrs. Jessup was a delightful old bird, who was frequently found dozing in a chair as she oversaw the young lady. They had some of the finest accommodations. No expense had been spared as Victor brought his letters of credit to the banks and introduced himself to the principles. He asked for recommendations on places to stay near the farms he intended to visit and further inquired about the people he had been advised to purchase horses from.

"That man is well known for putting nettles in the feed for his horses," Abigail whispered to Mel a few days later as they looked at the many horses presented to Victor at one of the farms they were visiting to view potential purchases.

Startled, Mel looked down at the petite girl, and she nodded sagely.

"He isn't to be trusted."

Mel, unable to tell her father while he conducted business, watched the groom, who held the lead ropes on several horses. He appeared innocent. You would never have suspected him of such behavior, but she believed her friend implicitly. Later, Abigail would confide that the man simply moved on when he had been found behaving improperly back in England. No one knew where he had gone. "Do you think he recognized you?" Mel worried as they ate dinner in their hotel room while waiting for her father to return. Mrs. Jessup was already dozing on the settee, her own ample dinner finished.

"No, he wouldn't. I was too young, but as you know, children have big ears." She grinned, the dimples in her cheeks framing a well formed and aristocratic face.

Mel couldn't help but return the impish smile. "Yes, I overheard many things I shouldn't have over the years."

"Oh, yes," she agreed, nearly spilling her soup from her spoon as she used it to gesture.

"Careful there."

"I'm being so unladylike," Abigail admitted, quickly bringing the spoon to her mouth, so she wouldn't spill it on the tablecloth.

"No, being unladylike would be riding astride," Mel teased her, knowing no one in le bon ton (British high society) and referred to as *the ton* would be so bold as to ride like that, at least, not publicly. It annoyed her since she had to follow this edict, and she'd nearly been unseated when she went riding in London. Men patronizingly suggested that she ride a less spirited horse, if she couldn't handle it. It had angered her as she was an accomplished rider and certainly could handle the horse. It was just the damned sidesaddle riding that made her appear inept.

"Oh, wouldn't it though," she agreed, delighting in her friend. She was so refreshing, not at all like her old fuddy-duddy friends, who must always be proper. Several of them had stopped riding since they felt it was unladylike. One had confided that she heard riding was bad for the woman's body, if she intended to have children. Abigail put that down as an old wives' tale and hoped it wasn't true since she adored her twice-daily rides.

Mel waited up for her father after her friend and her friend's chaperone had retired, wanting to tell him what Abigail had confided.

He nodded thoughtfully; sure he had sensed something too. The man had been recommended to him as a groom for the stable, mostly because he was English, but now, he wouldn't be offering the man a position. In fact, he had been about to offer the man the opportunity to escort the purchased horses to England for him, but he would find someone more trustworthy.

The next day, Abigail once again proved useful, pointing out how one of the stallions Victor was so keen on would occasionally hold his leg oddly. That had been overlooked, and when he inspected the hoof to see if there was gravel in it, the horse had shied away, nearly kicking the American due to the pain in its hoof. The large sum of money Victor had offered for the stud was rescinded.

Victor arranged invitations for the young women to attend a local party, insisting they both have new gowns for the occasion.

"Oh, how fun!" Abigail exclaimed, thrilled for the opportunity.

"You don't go to many parties back in England?" her friend asked as the seamstress came to measure them. Mel watched the woman knowingly as the hand that measured her hips, waist, and then bodice touched her more often than was necessary. Surprised, Mel was also pleased to see an answering look in the modiste's eye. She nodded imperceptibly and turned back to the younger girl being measured by the woman's assistants.

"Of course, but so far, I've had to wear Mama's hand-me-downs as Father won't expend unnecessary monies for fripperies."

Mel was annoyed on her friend's behalf. After all, the man spent hundreds of pounds on the horses and had been quite successful in his bets from what she could see. Their estate was well taken care of and prospering, but his gambling could easily turn on him, although he didn't appear to lose very often from what she had seen.

"A whole new dress though," she clapped her hands together joyfully. She was feeling every bit of the seventeen-year-old girl she was, and the excitement of a new dress was something unfamiliar in her experience.

"There you are, mademoiselle," the Belgium seamstress said as she finished measuring Mel, her hand lingering for only a second longer than necessary on the woman's bosom as they shared a look. "This will look trés magnifique when I finish it for you."

"I will not wear a corset, and you must make it so I can remove it myself. I do not travel with a maid," she told the woman meaningfully as they exchanged looks.

Abigail wondered why Mel didn't travel with a maid. It wasn't as if her father couldn't afford it. It would certainly be helpful to have someone lay out her clothes for her, pick up after her, and help her dress daily.

Mel stepped down from the stool she had stood on for her measurements. She felt it was quite unnecessary with her height, but the woman had insisted. "We will want to see your selection of fabrics. Do you have samples or bolts with you?" she asked the woman.

"Oh, non, mademoiselle. You will have to choose at my shop. I'm sorry, but I didn't bring any with me," she answered, sounding sincere.

Mel knew she lied, and the assistants exchanged startled looks. Mel had seen the assistants from the window as they entered the hotel carrying in bolts of fabric. Still, she knew the game that was afoot and would accommodate the woman. She nodded once and said, "I'll be by

on the morrow then." Her own French was the product of one of her tutors and the time she had spent in New Orleans.

"We could ride," Abigail stated, showing she understood a little of the quick French they had been speaking as the assistant hurried to finish her measurements.

"Oh, you need not come. I am certain Miss Lawrence can choose for both of you?" the seamstress tried to sound offhand, as though she was doing Abigail a favor.

"I would love to see what fabrics you have," Abigail responded, sounding enthused at the idea and not willing to miss out on the opportunity for her new dress, something she hadn't had back home too often. She was going to enjoy every moment of this exciting experience and was very grateful to Mr. Lawrence for the trip as well as the new clothing.

That was how they found themselves riding some borrowed horses when Mrs. Jessup would have much preferred a nice carriage. The groom accompanying them had a hard time keeping the older woman on her sidesaddle. Both younger women laughed boisterously at the dilemma, keeping far enough ahead that she couldn't admonish them for their behavior but well in sight, so she could honestly say she was chaperoning them. Arriving at the modiste's establishment, they waited for the groom to help them down from the large horses, sliding into his arms as he caught them, steadied them, and immediately released them.

"In the future, we will rent a carriage," Mrs. Jessup harrumphed indignantly, straightening her clothing.

"We thought you would enjoy the outing," Abigail said innocently, her eyes sparkling mischievously up at Mel, who grinned in return.

Mel wasn't answerable to the woman but understood how trying it must be to keep up with this little vixen.

"Perhaps it isn't as easy to ride when you are older–" began Mel and realized her mistake instantly. Mrs. Jessup was not pleased to be referred to as *older*. She had agreed to chaperone Abigail as a favor to the earl and his lady. She was being paid well for her services, but she didn't need insults. "Yes, perhaps a carriage would have been a better idea," Mel amended, going into the establishment before the unhappy atmosphere around the older woman could escalate. Abigail followed her eagerly. She thought herself too old for a chaperone, but her father had insisted and since Mr. Lawrence was paying for this trip, he was also paying for her chaperone, chosen by her father. She felt Mrs. Jessup, while fine for a child, was much too old-fashioned and frumpy for a young woman of her age. She would have preferred to go about like Melissa Lawrence did, without a chaperone in attendance.

The fabrics on display were quite lovely, and the assistants brought out several more. Mel was able to choose instantly but hesitated, and the modiste insisted she come in the back while her assistants showed Abigail and her chaperone the fabrics and allowed them to make their choices.

In the back, the woman pulled Mel into an embrace, and Mel responded immediately. She explored the older woman's lips, feeling her lithe body against her own riding clothes and enjoying the feel. She was young and healthy, and it had been months since she had made love to a woman, so of course, she responded. The modiste loved the feel of this sturdy young woman against her and wrapped herself around the taller woman. Neither of them spotted Abigail, who had innocently followed Mel.

Abigail, initially shocked to see the two women kissing, quickly backed away from the scene. Only when she was certain they couldn't see or hear her did she turn around and return to where Mrs. Jessup was enviously feeling the more expensive fabrics. Abigail, her cheeks aflame at what she had witnessed, was now feeling an emotion she had never expected to feel…jealousy. She had other friends but had never made a friend like the American. Was she jealous over their friendship? She realized that no, it wasn't. She may be young and innocent, but she knew the jealousy was because she wished she could be in Melissa's arms like that. She hadn't ever thought of it before but having it in a tableau before her, she instantly realized what she felt for Melissa went beyond friendship. Her hands went to her burning cheeks as she gazed out the shop windows. What in the world was the matter with her? This wasn't natural. She should be looking for a beau, one that could better her situation and perhaps help her family. She knew her duty. Her friends and her family would be shocked if they learned her thoughts.

"I'm quite warm. I'm going to stand outside and wait," she announced to a startled Mrs. Jessup, who immediately went with her.

"Are you ailing?" she inquired solicitously, suddenly worried that her charge was coming down with something. Sir Baxter would never forgive her if something happened to his daughter.

"Weren't you warm in there?" Abigail asked her chaperone as she closed the shop door behind her firmly, wondering at what she had seen. Had Melissa known the woman before, or was this how someone who was *that way* behaved? She had been envious of the arms around the seamstress. She wanted to be with Melissa and kiss her like that. What did that make her? She had a lot to think about, and her cheeks

continued to flush as her thoughts raced. She waved the air around her face, hoping to cool it.

"Maybe we should head back to the hotel?" Mrs. Jessup fretted. She glanced at the groom still holding their horses and ready to assist them. She looked back as the door opened behind them, and Melissa joined them.

"Ready to go? Have you chosen your fabrics?"

"Oh, yes. Her selection was quite wonderful," Mrs. Jessup answered cheerfully. "I think we should be getting back?" she hinted broadly. If her charge was ailing, it was best to get her into bed as soon as possible.

"Absolutely," Mel said, obviously in a good mood and not seeing Abigail's flushed cheeks as she went to spring up into her saddle. She was annoyed there was no pommel as the groom quickly kneeled, so she had a step. She reached down to hold the reins of the other horses, so he could assist Abigail and then Mrs. Jessup into their saddles. It took much longer to get the older woman and her ample bottom settled in her sidesaddle.

Abigail didn't participate in the conversation as they rode their horses back to the hotel, listening as Mrs. Jessup and Mel discussed the various colors and fabrics available to them and how the dresses would look. "She promised they would have a fitting in a few days, and the dresses would be ready a day or so after that, in time for the party," Mel told them. Abigail watched her friend to see if there was anything different about her. Other than what she perceived as slightly swollen lips, there was nothing about the woman to indicate she had been passionately kissing the seamstress. She wanted to ask her questions and yet…didn't want to know.

That night at dinner, Victor discussed his day and the horses he had seen. Mel participated, not realizing how quiet Abigail was being. Mrs. Jessup, certain that her charge was ill since she picked at her dinner, insisted the young girl go to bed early. Tired, both Abigail and her chaperone left the table early as the father and daughter continued their conversation.

Listening to Mrs. Jessup soundly asleep on the trundle bed in their suite, her snores rather annoying that night, Abigail got up to use the water closet in their luxurious rooms and was alarmed to see Melissa sneaking the seamstress into her room. Startled, she could only stare from her place in the shadows as the two women hushed each other's giggles while touching each other and quickly closed the door to Melissa's rooms. The younger girl didn't get much sleep as she thought about what the two women might be doing. She couldn't quite understand what two women would do together besides kissing, but now, she wanted to find out. As a result of her sleepless night, she looked haggard the next morning, confirming her chaperone's worst fears that she was ailing.

"I'll keep her company while you go down and get a meal. Have them send up something light for her," Melissa offered generously to the worried chaperone.

Abigail, pleased to still be abed when she desperately wanted some more sleep, was surprised to find herself alone with her friend. She wondered if the modiste had snuck out the previous night or early this morning?

"So, what is really wrong with you?" Mel asked knowingly, looking at her friend in polite concern.

"I'm just tired. I didn't sleep well," she told her honestly, refusing to look up at her. She wanted to ask so much; her curiosity was piqued but something kept her from speaking. She suddenly felt uncomfortable around Melissa.

"Oh, I'm sorry to hear that," she said, sitting down at the end of the bed. "We have the party to look forward to, and of course, Father has more horses to look at. Won't that be fun?"

Abigail enjoyed the idea of the party and the first dress that would be made *just* for her, but now that she knew what the seamstress was and possibly what she and Melissa had done, it made her uncomfortable. She figured conversing about horses was a safe bet.

CHAPTER FOUR

Thinking back to that first dress of her very own made her think about the dozen or so dresses that Augustus had had made for her immediately after their wedding. Their dowdy designs were in line with his opinion of what a modest wife of an earl of his stature should wear, conflicting with the youth and vitality of his young wife, much less the designs of the day. That first dress, paid for by Mr. Lawrence, was firmly packed away in one of her trunks, but she didn't know where because she hadn't been allowed to wear it since her marriage.

Augustus snorted in his sleep as he rasped out his last breaths; at least, she hoped they were his last. They sounded so painful as he drew another. Abigail wondered how long this agonizing ending would be. She had already been sitting here and holding his hand for hours. The doctors had come and gone, some almost resentfully, while others appeared to be ghoulishly anticipating the earl's death. It was obviously taking much longer than they anticipated. She had thought that none of them would want to miss this, but as the hours crept slowly by, they had taken turns keeping watch in case they were needed. She ignored them as they didn't deign to notice her, despite her position as his wife.

She sat back for a moment, easing the kink that was forming in her back and letting go of her husband's hand. She got up and stretched further, feeling hungry and worrying that her baby would need nourishment as well. She thought of her daughter but knew the nursemaid would not appreciate a visit this late at night. She was only allowed an hour a day to see her daughter, and she hadn't been allowed to breastfeed the little girl. Women of her station didn't do that, or so it was patronizingly explained to her. The implication was that someone of her intelligence couldn't possibly understand her position. She had never seen Augustus interact with their daughter. He had dismissed the infant once he knew it was a girl, deeming her not worthy of his time. He would provide for the child, of course, and he had named her, but other than that, he didn't see or have anything to do with the girl.

Without saying a word to the doctors that sat or stood while waiting for Augustus' demise, she went out into the hall. Seeing a servant standing there, perhaps waiting for word of the earl's passing to share with the other servants, she asked, "Could you have a dinner brought to me in the sitting room?" He looked startled, surprised that she would give him such an order. His slow response angered her. It was just another sign of the disdain the staff held her in. Finally, he hurried away to comply with her demand. She moved off to the other end of

the house, a long way from the master bedroom's suite of rooms, to look in on her daughter.

"Miss, you are going to wake the babe," the night nursemaid admonished her when she saw her there, trying to prevent her from entering the room.

"No, I will not," she contested, feeling a little stronger against the onslaught of insubordination that had reigned in this household since she had entered it. Treated as little more than a broodmare to her husband, she disliked almost all the servants under Mrs. Leister's command. "Get out of my way," she commanded the young woman, who was not much older than she. She fixed her with what she would later call a regal stare. She was, after all, an earl's wife, a countess, and the girl didn't dare directly thwart her. She knew there would normally be a discussion later, a disapproving conversation between Mrs. Leister and her husband, where he always sided with the long-standing housekeeper. He was certain she stayed with him out of absolute loyalty. Augustus would explain, condescendingly, why Abigail must not thwart the well-ordered household that his housekeeper ran and that she should accede to his wishes. She realized Augustus would never again tell her what to do, and she relished that idea. She pushed by the startled nursemaid and went to look at her daughter in the crib. A lit lamp was on a table nearby, and its low flame provided enough light that she could see the child. Already, she could see that Agatha looked like her with the blonde ringlets that would look beautiful as they grew, and with the pretty blue ribbons she would be adorable. With Augustus gone, Abigail would spend more time with her daughter, and these servants had better learn their place or they would be gone. She gazed at the child for an endless time, watching her suck her finger, her mouth working it as she had seen the child suck at her breast for the brief day she had been allowed to nurse before she had been taken to the woman Mrs. Leister had engaged to feed the earl's daughter. The wet nurse was long gone, having been discharged when Agatha turned two, the proper age for a young lady to be weaned and taught to eat solid foods. The resulting cries over this had broken Abigail's heart when she heard them, but there was nothing she could do as the decision wasn't up to her. Augustus had briefly talked about farming her out to another household in a few years, so she could be brought up properly. Abigail had worried about this and now realized it wasn't his decision anymore. No more would she have to obey Augustus' rather old-fashioned commands and demands.

She left her daughter's nursery, the nursemaid behind her huffing through her nose at the interruption of her schedule with the child. The woman would probably go back to sleep on the daybed near the crib. Abigail wondered if Agatha would be allowed to sleep until she woke or if they woke her at a scheduled time. She would have to learn more of the routine now that she didn't have to answer to Augustus. She wondered how many other things she could change after his demise.

"Ma'am your dinner is in the sitting room," a servant told her disapprovingly. It was the middle of the night, and the kitchen had been closed. They'd waited for her, and it was getting cold. He led her to her husband's sitting room.

"Thank you," she said, hurrying into the sitting room where she found the men who were there, who had been sleeping on the couches and settees, sitting up and absentmindedly consuming her late dinner picking at it with their fingers, while discussing various topics. She stared at them, angry at their presumption in eating her meal and turned to the servant. "Fetch me another, and this time, make sure you bring it to *my* sitting room. Also, bring an assortment of offerings for these gentlemen." She gestured to the doctors who hadn't heard her or even noticed her chagrin over their eating her meal.

"Yes, ma'am," he said, wondering how angry the cook would be to again be woken at this late hour. Everyone was on edge with the earl failing; they all knew he was dying. Some slept without a care in the world, but others, like himself, were up and catering to the missus and those doctors. He was supposed to be keeping watch, so he could inform the others when the earl passed. Instead, he found himself fetching and carrying, and although it was his job, he resented it. Her ladyship should have eaten at a normal hour instead of in the middle of the night.

Abigail couldn't wait with the doctors in Augustus' sitting room. They looked at her curiously, almost as though she were one of the servants, so she went through the door to his bedroom, and the other two doctors inside looked up from where they dozed in the chairs by the fireplace. They looked annoyed at her for waking them and then ignored her. That suited her fine as she looked in again on Augustus. His breathing was even more labored, if that were possible, and he looked in pain. Why had they called her so early in the evening? Did they want her to watch the man suffer?

She looked at the man that was her husband. He had been kindly in his own way, but he was too old to be a vigorous lover, and she had hated his paternal and condescending attitude towards her. After her father's viciousness though, she had been relieved to leave his house and come here to be Augustus' bride. He had tried to be nice and kind, but he was too old to change his ways. He felt she should obey him

and his superior knowledge at every turn. Knowing that the alternative was a convent or being turned out from both her husband's and father's houses, she obeyed and complied with his every wish. She learned what he wanted from her, and while she found most of his ideas old-fashioned and out of synch with the times and more fitting for a long-ago day, perhaps his mother's, she knew better than to voice an opinion. Women were to be seen and not heard, much like children. She was an ornament on his arm and was not to stray too far from him at the parties they attended in case he had need of something. She knew she had disappointed him with the birth of a girl child. She rubbed her stomach unconsciously, wondering if this was the boy child he had wanted, his heir that he would never see. She suddenly wondered what Augustus had looked like as a child growing up and if he would pass it along to her children.

Agatha looked like her, she acknowledged that without too much of a thought, but what part of her daughter's makeup was from Augustus. What part of the child was from Augustus' Germanic mother whose name the child bore? She wondered at that briefly as she sat there. One of the servants poked his head into the room, made eye contact with Abigail, and she rose to go to the door.

"Ma'am your dinner is in your sitting room, and they are bringing a repast for these gentlemen," he said loud enough for the doctors to hear while dozing in the chairs. He nodded toward them, almost as though the repast was the servant's idea and not Abigail's. She swallowed her ire.

"Have them lay the food in my husband's sitting room for the other doctors," she said, using her upper crust voice to her advantage and seeing the servant respond to it automatically. "Gentlemen," she whispered, so as not to disturb Augustus' restless slumbers, "there are refreshments for you as you continue your vigils." She knew by wording it that way they would feel that their 'help' as it were in waiting for the earl's death would be appreciated. She left them and hurried along the hall to her own sitting room beyond the earl's sitting room where the men congregated. "Has anyone sent for the earl's solicitors?" she asked the servant who was following her, uncertain why she asked the question.

"No, ma'am. We thought after–" he began and was shocked when the lady stopped in her tracks.

"Send someone for his solicitors immediately! They need to be here upon the earl's passing."

"But ma'am, it's raining…" he began.

It was this type of arguing that always showed their contempt for her. Her requests should be answered immediately and without question. She fixed him with a glare. "Who do you think you are? I am Lady Worthington, and you will send for my husband's solicitors as I requested. If you do not think that you can comply with my wishes, perhaps you should seek employment elsewhere? Have four, no five grooms ready to bear my notes to my husband's solicitors, and I'll write them out before they leave."

He stared at her and wilted under her violet gaze. Thinking her to be a scatterbrained blonde ornament on her husband's arm, they had all treated her in this manner. Mrs. Leister would not like that the lady of the house was giving commands. There was certain to be a clash of wills, and he wouldn't want to be in the middle of it. He also didn't wish to lose his position in the household. Being a servant to the Earl of Worthington carried with it a certain amount of prestige. "Yes,

ma'am, right away, ma'am." He hurried off, relieved to be out of her presence as he went to wake some of the men to carry messages to the solicitors that had come several times to see the earl since he had been bedridden with his accident. Several annoyed men slogged off to find mounts in the stables, carrying their mistresses' tidings and riding through the rain to waken these important men. There were many unhappy people from the earl's household that night.

Abigail ate her meal, pleased to find the hot soup to her liking. Despite their contempt for her, the servants knew their jobs, and she was grateful for this. The food was superb, if sparse. She finished up, drinking the poor wine that she knew the servants reserved for her. It was not the rich and expensive wines her husband had been fed. She knew there was a distinct difference in what she had been given over the years to what her husband would accept at his table when he was at home. She had been shocked to find her fare much different when he went to check on his various properties including the mills that had been in his family for generations. She put down her glass, unhappy with the after flavor of the bad wine. Still, she was satisfied with the rest of the meal, from the soup to the toasted bread that had been cut so thin she was able to dunk it in her soup. No one was there to stop her or stare disapprovingly as she enjoyed the meal and her stomach settled. She quickly wrote her missives, pondering over the last one as the grooms waited for them. She gave special instructions to the last groom, asking him to wait for a reply or even better, to return with the man it was addressed to. She walked through her sitting room to her husband's and saw several of the doctors there still gorging themselves on the substantial repast that the servants had brought for them.

"Are you satisfied, gentlemen?" she inquired solicitously, wondering where they put it all. Several of them were quite rotund and had obviously been starving if their countenance didn't show the fact that that they had been shoveling in the repast laid out for them. She noted that the food was much more varied than hers and was probably of superior quality, including the wine they were quaffing. She knew the servants wouldn't have wanted the men insulted and only the best would come from the earl's stores for these honored guests. She didn't care; she was satisfied for now.

"Quite, my lady," one of them answered for them all. He looked at her curiously, wondering at the earl's choice in brides. She was not of a particularly distinguished family, although perhaps, Worthington had wanted to align his family to part of the Earl of Pembleton's extended family. Abigail Baxter and her father, Sir Anthony Baxter, were certainly not in the same class as the Earl of Worthington. Still, she was a pretty chit, if featherbrained if you could put stock in what people said about her.

Abigail nodded, not willing to stop and chat. She returned to her husband's room, the stifling heat making her want to open a window again. She knew they would all be shocked at her actions if she deigned to attempt to assert herself. She nodded coldly to the servant sitting in the chair and warming himself by the fire. She couldn't understand why they needed the fire. She was uncomfortably hot in this room and yet, they were acting like it was the middle of winter. She saw a healthy supply of wood near the fireplace, ready to be put on the flames and wondered if Mrs. Leister knew of this sinful waste. She knew her own rooms wouldn't have been given the same consideration but stifled that thought. She was here for Augustus. How much longer could the man linger on? His open-mouthed breathing was so sonorous in the still room. She wondered if he had always snored but had no idea since he had left her rooms quickly after having relations with her. She had never seen him naked and never had the desire to. Sitting down, she waited, thinking over her life, her past sins, and her possible future. She was quite frightened at the possibilities.

CHAPTER FIVE

Lord Augustus Ernst Baden Worthington, fifth Earl of Worthington, died in his sleep just as the rainstorm cleared away and the sun's rays came up over the horizon. Abigail watched in amazement, almost as though she saw his spirit leave his body through his mouth. He took one loud snort of a gasp in his unending snoring, almost choking on it, and then, no more noise came from him. The two doctors in the room that were nodding off by the fire jerked up and ran to the bed, nearly stumbling in their haste.

Abigail sat back in her chair. She hadn't slept and had ben staring at Augustus, listening absent-mindedly to the snores. She watched as one of the doctors brought a candle and a mirror and put the mirror before his mouth. It did not fog up. They checked his pulse

twice…once by his neck and once at his wrist. There was no pulse. He was gone, and they looked at her sadly, as if she didn't know.

"He's gone," they told her unnecessarily.

Abigail nodded once and attempted to rise. She had sat in the chair too long and her legs were wobbly. They thought it was caused by her grief, and one of them grabbed her elbow to help her rise. "Thank you," she rasped, her own throat dry from sitting there so long with no respite. Her late-night dinner was many hours ago. "You will make arrangements for his body?" she asked, nodding towards the now dead man in his bed.

"Madam, you must have your servants dress him in his burial clothes," one of the doctor's told her loftily.

"Lady," she corrected him automatically and drew herself up. It was time she stopped these men and the women beneath her from treating her in the manner they had become accustomed to. She was a lady, a countess, and dammit, she would be treated as such. She may be young, but at twenty-one, she was an adult. She'd borne one child, who was now over two years old, nearing three, and she would bear another one in the winter. Both were heirs to his lordship's estate, and she and they would be given the respect they were due. "I am Lady Worthington, Countess Worthington, and you would do well to remember that." She fixed a violet-colored eye on him in a regal stare, and he backed down, realizing his impertinence. He nodded frostily. So, the feather-brained wife of his lordship had fangs. He would take note of that.

Another doctor went to tell the other doctors, and Abigail went to the door to the outer corridor, knowing a servant would be there waiting. She opened it, not surprised to see more than one waiting at this early hour.

"His lordship has passed. Please inform the staff and have someone come to bathe his body and put him in his wedding finery. Have his body dressed in it and placed in the coffin he had made. I believe it is stored in the stables, and it is to be placed in the hall."

The two servants standing in the hall stared at her in surprise. Her voice had changed; it had become imperious. No longer was she apologetic when asking for anything. No longer was she the meek bride.

"What are you waiting for? Go!" she told them and was pleased when the two ran off, nearly stumbling in their desire to do what she had commanded. She knew she would have to keep on this way if she was to survive in this household.

"Lady Worthington, our job here is done," the doctor she had upbraided said behind her.

Abigail turned to look at him and saw the others standing beyond the sitting room door, looking in at her and obviously having been informed of her husband's demise. "You can go. You can all go," she told them. They nodded in acknowledgement, gathering their coats, hats, and canes and departing without another word to her. She watched them go from the doorway of her husband's bedroom and saw Mrs. Leister bearing down on her.

"Lady–" the woman began imperiously.

"Mrs. Leister. Have his lordship bathed and dressed in his wedding finery. I had one of the servants send for his coffin. I will want that laid out in the foyer, so the staff and our tenants can come and pay their respects. No one is to bother me until the noon hour, and then, I will

want a repast. This evening when the tenants have come and gone, I will sit and pray for my husband's soul throughout the night." Abigail told her firmly, having thought this out as she sat there those many hours.

"I don't think that his–" the woman began after a long pause. She had been shocked to be addressed this way. Lady Worthington had always cowed to her wishes as his Lordship believed the housekeeper's version of events. He relied on her and her judgement heavily.

Abigail continued as though the housekeeper hadn't interrupted. "Furthermore, send to the dressmaker. Tell her I will need a dress for my husband's funeral. She has my measurements. I no longer wish to be dressed as my husband's grandmother but in the current fashions. It should be black, as befits the occasion. If she wishes to send over a couple of designs or the fabric, that would be acceptable to me. When my husband's solicitors arrive, please make sure they are fed, but again, I am not to be disturbed until after the noon hour. See that they are made comfortable as they await me."

"Lady Worthington–" the woman attempted to interrupt once again, her tone imperious and not to be trifled with. Too long had she been given the power in this house, too long had she catered to the needs of the earl. He had been pleased with her work, finding no cause to find fault with her work or the servants she directed over the years. She wouldn't allow this little upstart of a girl to upset her carefully crafted domicile.

"*Furthermore*, in the future, all decisions will come from me," she continued once again as though Mrs. Leister hadn't interrupted. "The earl is dead, and I will tolerate no further insubordination from the staff. Do I make myself understood, Mrs. Leister?" She stood there

and stared the woman down, her husband's body cold in his bed not fifteen feet from where they were standing.

The woman looked beyond her into the bedroom and could see the earl as the sun was shining in through the windows. Despite the bed hangings, he looked frail and very, very pale. He was certainly dead, and this little girl presumed to give her commands? She drew herself up to full height, taller than Abigail by a couple of inches.

Abigail had thought of this moment throughout the night. She knew that Mrs. Leister wouldn't give in gracefully, and she was prepared for her. "Do you like your position, Mrs. Leister?" she asked conversationally, eyeing the woman to watch her reactions.

"Why, of course, the earl said...."

"The earl is dead," she reminded her quietly, "and I am not." They stared at each other, each attempting to gain the upper hand. "If you wish to leave your position with the earl, go..." she continued offhand and watched as the woman's eyes flared. "I will write a letter of recommendation; however, I do hope you will stay as you really are the best person for the job."

Mrs. Leister wasn't sure what to say. Was she being threatened with losing her position? She'd never be able to hold her head up again. Still, the suggestion of a letter of a recommendation and then the compliment that she was the best person for the job had its effect. "N...no, ma'am. I would like to keep my position," she assured her. Her voice was taking on a different tone as she realized this woman, this girl really, was actually in control of this house...at least, until the solicitors came and her father took over. She could play the game until the twit was put back in her place. Let her enjoy her feeling of power

for a few hours at least. She hadn't survived all these years and risen to this position to be put out by this…this…feather-brained child!

Abigail saw the narrowed eyes of her nemesis and realized this was only a temporary truce. The woman would have to be replaced if Abigail was to maintain any semblance of control, but that could be handled later. She had to prepare her husband for his funeral. "We will have my husband's funeral three days hence. Have the minister call on me this afternoon or tomorrow at his convenience." She knew the man would pee himself trying to get here at all costs. The Earl of Worthington was a benefactor of his esteemed church, and he couldn't afford to lose his main source of income by insulting the man's wife, no matter how he felt about the young woman. "I am going to rest, and I am not to be disturbed. Is that understood?" she asked, and at the woman's nod she turned, looked at Augustus once more, and walked firmly to the bed to remove the Worthington crest from his finger. The housekeeper looked on aghast at her actions.

There was no heir to the earl's title. What would become of them all? A distant cousin would inherit the title as little Lady Agatha could not. What the new earl would do with them all was really in question, and Mrs. Leister narrowed her eyes contemplatively. She would ingratiate herself with the new earl, show him how invaluable she really was, and this…this feather-brained twit—a moniker she had unknowingly given the woman and which spread to the other servants and those who worked for the earl—would be out on her backside. Still, as the mother of Lady Agatha, she supposed the new earl would make accommodations for her, and there was a house on the estate that the Dowager Countess of Worthington could live in. She watched as Abigail removed the ring, a family heirloom that should go to the next earl, and then turned and went through the door to the master's sitting room.

Abigail locked the door to her sitting room for the first time in her life while living in that house. She knew it was a childish antic as Mrs. Leister had the keys to all the rooms in the house. The keys should have been turned over to Abigail as lady of the house and then symbolically bestowed upon the housekeeper, but Augustus hadn't done that. Instead, the way he handled it elevating the housekeeper to the same status of his wife and lowering his wife's status to that of a servant. She quickly undressed for bed, feeling the cooling room which, as she had thought, didn't have an adequate supply of wood in it. She hurried to get under the covers, the down comforter quickly enveloping her as her warmed body helped heat the cocoon she made for herself. She was tired from her vigil of watching over her husband that night, and she knew keeping it up for the following night would wear on her, but she was determined that the gossip, and there would be gossip, would show that she was a good and loyal wife to the earl.

Abigail tried not to think any more about what would come in the following days. She had thought it all through the previous night, the hours dragging as she thought about what she would do. It was not going to be easy, and she wasn't happy with her thoughts, but she was determined.

CHAPTER SIX

The butler had barely answered the front door for the twelfth time when Sir Baxter lumbered in. "So, the old earl has passed away?" he asked the butler as he handed him his hat, his cane, and then waited for the man to help him off with his coat.

"Indeed, sir," the man said loftily. He thoroughly disliked his lordship's father-in-law. The man was a bore and even more of a boar in appearance with his rotund body. He had appeared frequently in the beginnings of the marriage between his lordship and Lord Baxter's daughter. Essentially, he wanted to admonish his daughter for not becoming pregnant immediately, but mostly, he was there to ask the earl for another loan. His appearances had lessened once Augustus had refused him anymore money. Still, he liked people to think he was good friends with his lordship, a far superior name than his own.

"Where is my daughter?" he asked, seeing that Lord Worthington was laid out in a coffin, flowers from their hothouse already placed around him on display. A servant, probably a groom, scuttled away from paying respects to the earl upon seeing Lord Baxter staring at him.

"Her ladyship has left word not to be disturbed–" began Mr. Franklin.

Lord Baxter could hear murmurs coming from the study. "Are his lordship's solicitors here?" he asked, interrupting the servant.

"Yes, your lordship–" he began again, annoyed with the dismissal as the man waddled across the hall and opened the door.

"Gentlemen…" Lord Baxter greeted them and closed the door behind himself. Half an hour later, he made his way up the stairs and asked a passing servant, "Where is her ladyship's room?"

Directed to Abigail's bedroom, he was annoyed to find the door locked, and he pounded on it. "C'mon girl, get yourself up and downstairs where you belong!"

Abigail, having only gotten a few hours' sleep, shook herself groggily awake as she heard her father at her bedroom door. She considered not answering it but knew it would only get worse as he created a scene. She was frightened but didn't dare ignore him. She quickly got up, grabbing her wrap to cover her in the cool room, the fire having gone out completely due to the inadequate supply of wood. Unlocking the door, she peered out at her father, the light in the hall telling her it was near the noon hour. "Father? I gave word…."

"It's time to be up and about. How dare you let your servants greet your guests? What will people think?"

"I was up all night with–"

"Furthermore, your husband's solicitors are here waiting for you. How rude to keep these important men waiting for your convenience," he sneered, brushing past her and looking about the well-appointed bedroom. Worthington had merely had his mother's rooms cleaned for his bride, but quality was quality, and it showed with the silk-lined walls and antique furniture.

"I know. I sent for them before Augustus–" she began but was interrupted once again.

"Well, we've come to an understanding about how to manage Worthington's estate. Of course, you'll be taken care of as well as your daughter." His tone disparaged the word 'daughter,' making it sound like a defect. He was thrilled when he learned nothing in the wording of Worthington's will said the new earl would get the immense fortune behind his properties. They could sell off some of the properties, providing more monies for the Baxters. "They have some things for you to sign...."

"Father, I should dress," Abigail put in weakly, already exhausted at the thought of dealing with her father and the solicitors. She was annoyed that her father assumed she would blindly follow his wishes. She knew he would funnel off as much money as Augustus had, leaving nothing for her and her children. She could feel her stomach roiling slightly, her morning sickness about to come upon her now that she was awake.

Anthony Baxter looked at his daughter distastefully. He had lost all respect for her upon finding her in the arms of another woman. Thank God that hadn't gone much beyond his own family's shame. Of course, he had explained it to Lord Worthington. After all, it was only fair that the old earl learn what kind of woman he was marrying. He had been grateful for the payment of his debts but had been confused when the man stopped lending him funds in order to pay his new debts. Now, the entire fortune of the Worthington Estate was at his hands and his daughter was worrying about her dress? He looked at her, disheveled from sleeping and her hair in disarray, and frowned disapprovingly. "Yes, get yourself ready for the day. I will wait downstairs with the others for you to sign their papers. Don't be long. I'll give you fifteen minutes," he told her imperiously.

Abigail stared after her father as he abruptly left her room. He wouldn't listen to her; she already knew that from her past experiences with him, and her mother wasn't there to act as a buffer. He would bully her into signing whatever paperwork the lawyers had for her to sign, whatever he saw fit for the estate. She didn't even know what it entailed and had hoped to hear what the solicitors had to tell her. She shut the bedroom door and pulled on a rope to call for a servant.

"Yes, ma'am?" the servant who stuck her head in inquired solicitously.

"I'll want my breakfast brought up to me. Has Mr. Adams arrived?"

"Mr. Adams, ma'am?"

"Yes, a Mr. Adams. I sent for him last night when the other solicitors were sent for."

"I'll inquire, ma'am," she promised and hurried out before Abigail could ask anymore of her.

Abigail was annoyed. She wasn't to be referred to as ma'am. She was her ladyship or countess, and that was going to have to change. She wanted to stamp her foot but knew that was the action of a spoiled brat. Her father was already causing a bad mood, and she needed to keep her head about her. She hoped Mr. Adams had come. She needed him desperately for the plan she had formulated for hours last night to come to fruition. She needed a man, or rather men, who would obey her, not questioning her and resisting everything she said. She knew what kind of men the solicitors were. They were older men, who had catered to the earl and would have very similar views and attitudes to his. They were men like her father, who were bullies. She knew he was salivating over the earl's vast fortune, and she was going to save it for herself in order to raise her children. She patted her stomach, necessitating a run for the slop jar in order to throw up the few contents of her stomach.

It had been a lot longer than the fifteen minutes her father had allotted her when Abigail made an appearance downstairs. She was dressed in the most matronly dress she owned, dark gray and not the black she knew she should be wearing. But no matter what she wore, she knew her father would disapprove. She didn't stop in her husband's study, instead choosing the room she had arranged for Mr. Adams, where he would be alone and away from the solicitors or those who had come to pay respects to her husband. She had come down the servants' stairs at the back of the house, so no one would see her. The servants who had seen her, immediately resented her presence in their midst, but she ignored them as she made her way carefully through the second floor to the comfortable little sitting room.

"Mr. Adams," she said by way of greeting, holding out her hand to him.

Adams rose from where he had been daydreaming on a settee, taking her ladyship's hand in his own and kissing the back of it. He wondered why he had been summoned, wishing her note asking him to come immediately had further elaborated. He didn't really know the earl and had no idea why he was here, and it was obvious that people had been coming to pay their respects. The servants had at first led him to one of the rooms where food was served to some of the people who had come to extend their condolences. He had seen the team of solicitors that had been ushered into the earl's study, some he knew by name. He was there when Lord Baxter arrived, a disagreeable man from what he had seen at the tracks, if ever there was one. He understood that Lady Worthington was Baxter's daughter, and he frowned a little, wondering why he was here.

"I am sorry to keep you waiting. I was up all night, you understand…" she began apologetically. "Please, sit, sit," she said, waving him to a chair.

"Lady Worthington, I do not understand why you summoned me?" he began hesitantly. He had no idea why a woman of her station would send him a note.

"I believe you are the manager for Miss Lawrence here in England?" she began in return.

He lifted his brows in surprise. "Yes, my lady, I am." He remembered now. Melissa Lawrence had been friends with Lady Worthington back when she was just Lady Baxter. There had been a hint of some scandal, but few knew the truth.

"She must trust you implicitly to have you overseeing her affairs here in England," she stated.

He inclined his head modestly. "I believe it was she who recommended me to her father, and then, when he passed away…" he left off. After all, the earl had just passed away as well.

"So, you must be a clever fellow to handle things from half a world away. I understand Melissa is in Australia now?"

Was this a social call? he wondered. He couldn't understand her nattering on about Melissa Lawrence, his employer. "Yes, she has started a ranch down there. They call them stations."

Abigail knew that from her last letter, and she knew that Melissa had married. She wanted to ask about that but didn't know if this man knew of the marriage. Melissa had asked her to keep that quiet, so she would. "I am wondering if you can take on other clients?"

"Other clients, my lady?"

"Yes, my husband has just passed away, and I will need some help maintaining his affairs."

If he had been hit upside the head, he couldn't have been more flabbergasted. "I'm certain he will have directed his solicitors how to take care of you and his affairs after he was gone."

"I'm sure he did," she said agreeably. "However, I'm also certain that I'm going to need a solicitor…perhaps, a few of them," she waved towards the door in the general direction of her husband's study, "in order to protect my and my children's interests. I am going to need someone *on my side*, you understand?"

Adams did understand, very well. Victor Lawrence's carefully constructed will had left his entire estate to his daughter, and in a time when men ruled over their women, it was a very unusual situation. He couldn't imagine that Lord Worthington had left it to chance or to a mere woman to handle his affairs. He would bet those five lawyers in her study were even now going over his last will and testament.

"My father, as you know, will have his say in this matter as well. I would like to hire you to help me find a team of solicitors, who will make sure my husband's wishes in this matter are carried out. He wished his children to be taken care of, and I don't wish my father to get his hands on the money he left for them."

Now, he understood. Lord Baxter's gambling was well known. He could see the sense in that and nodded. He had had to hire and fire several lawyers on Miss Lawrence's behalf over the years because they simply couldn't understand working for a woman. "Yes, my lady, I understand," he told her. "You wish to retain my services to find solicitors who would be willing to work on your behalf and possibly against your husband's solicitors and your father?"

"I wish to retain your services for that, yes, and there will possibly be more at a future date," she told him cryptically. "Time is of the essence, and if Melissa Lawrence trusts you, I will trust your judgement and your honesty implicitly. My father has already stated they have papers for me to sign, and I don't wish to sign anything until my solicitors have reviewed them and given their approval."

He realized a lot more now and nodded again. He was honored that she would trust him with this information.

"I'm going to confide in you, Mr. Adams. You must not tell another soul as they might accidentally use this information in the...negotiations we are about to enter into?" She waited for his nod again before she continued. "I am with child again. My husband knew of it, and we hoped for a son and heir. If this is the long sought for son and heir, he is the next earl. I do not wish to be plagued with the worry

of what the next earl in line for the title will do while I wait out my confinement with my child." She caressed her stomach for emphasis, not even realizing she was doing so as she spoke. "My daughter needs to be kept in the manner, which Augustus and I had planned. If a new earl is sought before we know whether this child is a boy or a girl, the stress may cause me to miscarry."

Mr. Adams realized the implications immediately. In a patriarchal society such as England's, the child, if it were a boy, would receive the lion's share of the estate. Lady Worthington would be kept until the child was twenty-one years of age. The young lady would probably have been bartered to a good marriage to some man of equal status to herself. He nodded again, realizing the dilemma that Lady Worthington was in. She was at the hands of some very powerful solicitors and her father, and her sex was working against her. They both knew that Lord Baxter's probable motives were not for the welfare of his daughter or granddaughter. "I understand, my lady. I have several solicitors at my disposal that I have used for Miss Lawrence's affairs. These solicitors understand that working with a woman is to their benefit, their *financial* benefit," he emphasized.

Abigail understood him completely. Most men wouldn't do anything if they couldn't profit from it. That made sense to her. She knew her husband's solicitors not only made money at his expense but wielded a lot of power because of it. She didn't want them to have power over her. "Can you get them here quickly? I think I can delay the reading of the will for a day or two, but I daren't do more or my father and those men will think me unable to make a decision."

They both knew that having Lady Worthington declared incompetent would place her father in complete control of not only herself but also her husband's estate. Her daughter was far too young to matter, and unless the child she carried were a boy, it would suffer the same fate. However, even if it were a boy, once Lord Baxter had the estate in his clutches, there might not be anything left for the boy to inherit when he came of age. "Yes, I believe I can have them here shortly. I will leave immediately and see to this myself. They will want to see a copy of the will," he warned her. He wondered at the rumors about her being the flighty wife of the Earl of Worthington. He saw none of that at this moment. She seemed steady and ready to do battle against the men who would keep her subjugated. He himself was married to a strong woman, who he hoped would be able to cope with or without him. He was just grateful she wanted to go through life with him as her husband. He admired strong women, and in Melissa Lawrence he had an admiring gratitude because she had enabled him to do a job he enjoyed and would continue to do for her to the best of his ability. If he could help her friend, he would.

"I'll see that receive a copy when they arrive," she promised, not sure how she could do that when the men were already ensconced in her husband's study with it. Her father had probably reached an accommodation with them to make sure she stayed in line with their thoughts on how it should be administered. She could already feel the noose of servitude tightening around her neck, if she allowed her father to have his way, but she wouldn't allow it. She'd go down fighting, and she truly hoped she could ward him and the other solicitors off until this man and the men he hired on her behalf were able to save her.

"Then I will leave you, Lady Worthington, and I will see you again in a few days. I am sorry for the death of your husband."

"Thank you, Mr. Adams," she told him and allowed him to take her hand again as he took her leave. She wanted him gone. The sooner he was gone, the sooner he would come back. She slipped out behind him and made her way to the front salon, which was full of people wishing to pay their condolences and be seen. If they hadn't already left a card and viewed the earl laid out in the hall, they would upon leaving. She spent the next half hour murmuring her gratitude to various people for coming. Many would go to the church to pay their respects there to and be seen.

CHAPTER SEVEN

"I told you to meet me in fifteen minutes," a voice rasped in a whisper at her ear, not wishing to be overheard.

If Abigail didn't immediately recognize the threatening voice, she certainly recognized the hand grasping her arm firmly. She turned to her father, knowing he wouldn't want to make a scene. "I thought you would be in here," she gestured to the few people who remained in the salon.

Annoyed with his daughter, he shook his head. Of course, he had meant the study. Hadn't he made that clear upstairs? He couldn't remember, but it had certainly been much longer than the fifteen minutes he had given her. It had been hours, necessitating his going upstairs again to discover she was gone from her rooms. Asking a passing servant, he learned she had been downstairs for over an hour.

He was furious that she had kept him waiting. He was equally embarrassed and angered that she had kept such important men waiting. "Your solicitors are waiting in your husband's study. They came at your behest and have been waiting many hours. That's very rude, me gal," he told her, trying to keep his voice low and his anger in check. He suppressed the urge to shake her. It wouldn't do for the curious, who had come to pay their respects, to spread gossip about his dealings with the widow, even if she was his daughter.

"Of course, Father. I didn't realize," she murmured, allowing him to pull her along, his pudgy fingers grasping the flesh of her arm painfully hard. She knew she would have bruises there later.

"Hurry along there, girl," he told her, wanting to give her a shove and a push but nodding coldly to some new arrivals as they crossed the great hall towards the study. "Here she is," he said in a loud and friendly voice as soon as they arrived in the study.

Five men looked up from the papers they had been reviewing. They'd gone over them many times, discussing them once with the Earl of Baxter and then amongst themselves as they waited and debated, not to mention the discussions that had taken place when the papers were drawn up.

"Lady Worthington," several acknowledged her as the men all got up to bow to her, one or two calling her, "Countess Worthington."

Abigail acquitted herself as she curtsied respectfully in return. "Gentlemen, I do apologize for keeping you waiting. I was up all night with my husband, God rest his soul."

"God rest his soul," several of them repeated.

"With all my guests offering their condolences, it has been difficult to find a moment alone. My father graciously reminded me that you

were waiting. I hope my servants have kept you well supplied?" She glanced at the crumbs of food she could see on trays that had been brought in. Unobtrusively, she pulled her arm from her father's clutching fingers.

"Lady Worthington, your father and we have come to an understanding regarding Lord Worthington's estate. We have the preliminary paperwork drawn up for you to sign acknowledging..." the man droned on, and at some point, Abigail stopped listening. He seemed to be the spokesman for all the men standing there and watching her reaction as they essentially told her what had been her worst fears. Her father would have custody of her and her daughter, and he would administer the estate for her. She realized right then that he was appropriating all the earl's possessions, including herself, under the guise of protecting her and her daughter. "If you would just sign here?" he asked politely, ready to hand her the quill pen, the papers before her on the desk.

"Sir, would you ask anyone to sign papers before they had read them and understood them?" she asked him, trying to sound agreeable and pleasant. Inside she was quaking with fear. He had sounded so reasonable when he asked her to sign that she felt compelled to just sign where he told her to.

"But Lady Worthington, I just explained..." he began condescendingly.

"Abigail, just sign those papers," Lord Baxter barked at her.

Abigail looked at the six men looking back at her, judging her and waiting. She could feel the intimidation in the air as they all waited expectantly. She looked at the papers on the desk, the wax seal waiting nearby. They expected her to put the ring she wore on her hand, the signet ring that Augustus had given her, into the wax and onto the documents once they were signed. "May I read–?" she began, sounding hopeful.

"For Christ's sake, Abigail. Sign the papers!" her father barked again.

Abigail was looking at the papers and the wax, and she looked up in time to see the other men start at the words her father had used. He always seemed angry. She could remember back to a time when her mother had been a buffer between the children and his anger. She wondered if it was his tremendous losses that had caused this anger. She turned slightly to face him, never so afraid in her life. He had been known to be violent on occasion. Her brothers had well known the adage of spare the rod and spoil a child. She turned away, too afraid to confront him at this moment. "Is this the paper you would have me sign?" she verified, hoping to get some sort of inspiration before she signed it.

Lord Baxter expelled air through his nose in a loud gush, obviously angered over her flighty sounding question.

"Yes, my lady. If you'll sign there," one of the solicitors pointed to the paper where she should sign, trying to hand her the pen.

Abigail got the strangest feeling that if they could, the men would put the pen in her hand, dip the ink, and sign it with their hand firmly around hers forming the letters and signing away her rights. She spotted other papers and reached for them instead. "Is this my husband's will?" she asked, trying to keep her voice steady.

"You don't need–" began Anthony, his annoyance over her delay in signing the paperwork that they had carefully drawn up in accordance with his desires was obvious. They had followed the Earl of

Worthington's wishes, but only to a point. Her signature, once it was obtained, altered things considerably and profitably for the lesser earl.

"Yes, my lady. As you can see this is the original in his own handwriting."

Abigail held out her hand for the document, so she could look at it. It was written out three and half years ago according to the date. It was right before their marriage…no, it was right afterward. His hand was much stronger then, and the lines were written without the spidery crawl he developed in later years. There were several pages attached.

"And these are our copies that repeat the Lord Earl's wishes," he continued helpfully, hoping by accommodating her ladyship, she would sign the documents, and they could all go home. It had been a long day, and they had been bullied into creating that other document by Sir Anthony. They were all tired and had been well fed, but they had other work to attend to. He held up his copy to show her.

Abigail took the copies in hand and picked up the papers they wished her to sign, glancing at them. She held them firmly in her left hand, stacking them there as she looked up with a pleasant smile on her lips. "I thank you all for coming, gentlemen. I will look these over and let you know when I'm ready to sign them. I am sure you understand with Augustus newly deceased that I need some time to mourn. I must see to more of the arrangements. I will see you all at the funeral," she assured them, taking a sidestep as she heard her father behind her and easily turning away, so he couldn't grasp her arm again. She hurried to the door, the paperwork firmly in her hand and was out the door, leaving six stunned men behind her. They hadn't expected her to read the paperwork they had asked her to sign.

"What…?" began one of the other men.

"I thought…" another began.

"She took…"

"I'll straighten her out on this and get you those signed papers," Anthony assured them. He had worked too hard for too long to get to this point to have that little–. He shook his head at his own thoughts, angry beyond reason. If she would just sign the damned paperwork! He left them to go find his daughter as they all exchanged looks. There really was no rush for Lady Worthington to sign, but they had thought it would be concluded as Lord Baxter assured them. They gathered up the remaining copies of the paperwork and slowly filed out of the earl's study. The butler hurried to get their coats, gloves, and canes and call for their carriages.

Abigail knew her father would be looking for her. She rolled the large sheaf of paperwork she had managed to abscond with and kept them tightly in her grasp. She did want to read it all, so she could understand what exactly Augustus had left her and her children. She wanted to know the extent of all he owned, having not known during their marriage because Augustus didn't want to worry 'her pretty little head' as he termed it. She wondered where she could hide everything as she made her way upstairs quickly. She knew her room would be searched, if not by her father personally, then at his direction by the servants. She headed for her husband's bedroom, making certain none of the servants were around as she slipped inside.

The bed had been remade with clean sheets, but the room still smelled of death. She hurried to his dressing room and slipped the sheaf of papers inside a box near the door, marking it in her mind as she turned determinedly towards the windows to open one. They were stuck. It was almost as though they had never been opened before. She tried several windows before one of them moved slightly, and the wind immediately blew the drapes aside. The cold came in through the window, and she shivered, closing her eyes for a moment as she thought about the coming days.

"My lady?" a voice asked at the door, one of the maids looking at her in surprise.

"This room stinks of death," she answered, feeling defensive about the window she had opened. Last night's storm was long gone, and the day was sunny but very windy. "Help me get these other windows open, and if you can't do it, fetch a footman. I want my husband's room aired," she told her in the firm voice she was adopting. She knew the woman would not only fetch a footman but also Mrs. Leister. She watched as the woman tried and failed to open the windows, finding them as tightly shut as she had. She watched nervously, feeling almost as though the woman knew she had just stashed the paperwork. "Fetch a footman," she reminded the maid, who looked up in surprise, nodded, and hurried out. Abigail was certain Mrs. Leister would make an appearance, and she wanted to wait for her, but she didn't want to be caught in her husband's rooms.

Abigail left the room and ran into another maid. "Oh, my lady. The dressmaker is here."

"Have her attend me in my sitting room," she said, trying to make her voice calm, but her heart was fluttering as she nodded to the maid and turned to head down the hall.

The dressmaker curtsied to her as she brought in several bolts of fabric. "I want this dress made quickly, you understand," Abigail told her. "I do not want the old-fashioned designs my husband chose for me, but I also don't want it to be gaudy. I want it to look fashionable but completely respectful of my husband's station."

"I understand, my lady. Of course, my lady," she responded as they quickly went over the appropriate fabrics for a funeral, choosing a silk that would look fitting and give the proper elegance to the widow. "I would suggest one of these designs," she hesitantly offered Abigail, showing her several sketches.

Abigail was pleased as the designs were neither old nor fuddy duddy. She wouldn't look at all like her ancient and long-deceased mother-in-law. She nodded as she pointed to a sensible but stylish design.

"I'll have my girls get to it immediately, madam," the dressmaker promised her, hurrying out, so she could get started. She had three girls working for her, and they'd have to work around the clock to make the gown for her ladyship, but she knew how important it was. She too agreed that a new and stylish gown was what the widow needed. She had never agreed with his lordship's designs but had followed them faithfully since he was the one paying for the gowns he ordered for his wife.

Abigail mused, looking out the windows of her sitting room as she took a deep breath, glad to know the paperwork was hidden. She could see several of the tenants making their way to the mansion and going in through the side doors to make their way to the hall and pay their respects. Several coaches made their way ponderously up the long drive, and she pulled back from the window, so she wouldn't be seen.

There would be enough gossip going around as there always was in their community.

Abigail thought back to the party she and Melissa had attended in Belgium. She was grateful to have Mrs. Jessup help her with the dress, the first party dress she had ever owned that was solely her own. She had admired herself in the full-length mirror in their suite, and she was pleased to see how grown-up she looked. She wondered if Melissa would notice her. She also wondered if the seamstress she had seen Melissa kissing had been back to their suite. She had gotten up at every sound the past few nights but had seen nothing.

Abigail put her shawl around her shoulders, and Mrs. Jessup hurried to fetch her own. She stopped in the living room of the suite to see Melissa in a dark blue velvet gown. She looked stunning in her own way, the dark color not at all like the pastel colors Abigail had chosen for her own dress. Melissa was so grown up, but at over twenty-one, she supposed the young woman could choose her own colors. Girls of Abigail's age always wore pastels. She couldn't wait to get married someday or become old enough to choose rich colors such as the blue velvet that looked so fine.

"Wow, you look stunning," Mel said to her friend with a smile.

"I do?" she asked, looking down at her dress as though searching for a stain. She wondered what Melissa saw in that seamstress and what she saw when she looked at Abigail. She probably thought her a child.

"You do indeed," Mr. Lawrence assured her, coming out of his room and trying to fasten his cufflinks. "Melissa, would you help me here?" he asked in a grouchy, teasing sort of voice.

Mel laughed at her father's attempts to dress himself. "You should have brought a man servant."

"I told you, I don't need–" he began but caught the twinkle in her dark brown eyes and laughed with her. He did need a man servant, and she should probably have a lady's maid, but she was far too independent and insisted she didn't need one hanging about and doing things she could do herself. He watched as she attached the cufflinks that had been a gift from his wife, her mother, and marveled that this was his daughter. Her gown was fabulous, but she looked...odd in it. He almost felt as though she would look better wearing the suit he was wearing. Still, it wasn't her fault she looked like his side of the family and was not her genteel mother. He smiled fondly at her as she finished attaching the jewel at his cuff.

"There you go, Father. Hurry and get your jacket on, so we can go," she urged him.

He saluted her, and they both laughed as he went back into his bedroom to fetch the required item.

"Are we ready to go?" Mrs. Jessup asked as she exited the bedroom she shared with Abigail.

"Just," Mel told her; glad she didn't wear old ladies' clothes as this matron did. Mrs. Jessup looked frumpy and had far too much lace in her old-fashioned frock. Mel loved the blue of her velvet gown but knew it didn't quite suit her. The style was fashionable, and she looked nice, but it just wasn't quite...her.

"Ready, ladies?" Victor asked as he surveyed the three women he would be escorting to the party. Glancing at Mel again, he wished he had given her some of her mother's jewelry, thinking maybe that would help the overall appearance, then stopping himself. There was nothing wrong with Mel's appearance. She stood proudly next to him, and to his surprise, she almost matched him in height and girth. The petite

Lady Abigail looked positively delicate next to his robust daughter. Mrs. Jessup looked fine in her own way, and he shared a smile with her over their charges' heads as he escorted them out. Four men-at-arms had been hired for the evening to escort them to the party. They would be riding along at the sides of their carriage, their swords and pistols at the ready to defend the family should it become necessary.

The party, a small gathering of merely one hundred people, was set in a distinctly French Colonial home. Shaped in a C pattern, its yellow gold exterior looked wonderful in the setting sun, almost as though it were a painting nestled against the green hills. Their hosts, Count and Countess de Croÿ, were pleased to see the American, his daughter, and Lady Baxter. The count was always looking to expand his business contacts and found it fascinating to see how others controlled their wealth. The American, while holding no title, was rumored to be enormously wealthy. Seeing the American's daughter again, he was surprised at her beautiful gown, but he had heard his wife talk about the girl, who was twenty-one and not married, and he could see why. Still, there were those who would marry her for her father's rumored enormous fortune, which it was understood she would inherit someday as his only heir.

"Mr. Lawrence," the count greeted him, bowing slightly, his heels tapping together as he stood back at attention. "Allow me to introduce my wife, Countess de Croÿ."

"Count de Croÿ," Victor said charmingly, bowing to them both and taking the Countess' hand and kissing the back of it. "Countess de Croÿ. May I introduce my daughter, Melissa Lawrence, her friend, Lady Baxter, and the lady's chaperone, Mrs. Jessup."

"Charmant," he said, bowing first over Melissa's hand and then Lady Baxter's as his wife acknowledged the older woman.

They were led into the formal ballroom where people were standing about gossiping and waiting for the amusements to begin. The men and women had segregated, and the countess led Melissa and Abigail towards a younger group of girls, Mrs. Jessup trailing discreetly behind. She introduced them around and left them to attend to some of her other guests.

The women, girls really, talked rapidly in French, assuming the American and the Englishwoman wouldn't understand a word of it. Mel exchanged a look with Abigail and together, they turned their backs on the group and walked away.

"Excusez-moi," a young gentleman approached them.

Mel nearly laughed at his bad French and decided being straightforward might shock this *polite* society, but she wasn't going to let the young man be miserable as he was looking so hopefully at Abigail. "We speak English," she told him quietly.

He looked instantly relieved as he immediately bowed. "May I ask to be introduced to your chaperone?" he asked, looking hopefully towards Mel as though she had this title.

"Of course," Abigail said, a delighted smile of mischief on her face as she glanced at Melissa. She had been appalled at the few words of French she had caught from that group of Belgian girls. They had been rude towards Mel, who simply turned away. She caught it in time to turn with her, making it look as though both were of the same mind. She had to wonder how often Mel was insulted like that. "May I introduce you to my chaperone, Mrs. Jessup?" she said, giving it the French inflection.

The young man looked with surprise at the frowning matron several paces behind the two young women he had approached, but he quickly recovered as he bowed to her formally. "Madam, I would like to be introduced to your charge…s," he added belatedly, looking at Mel. She gazed at him as though his equal, and it alarmed him. She was taller than he!

Mel distinctly heard Mrs. Jessup mumble, "Impertinent," under her breath before she obliged the young man.

The title of lady delighted him as he gazed at the petite blonde, but he was surprised and confused by the title of Miss attributed to the large, young woman. Still, she was dressed expensively, which bespoke money. He glanced once more at Lady Baxter.

"May I ask for the privilege of the first dance?" he asked in what he hoped was a charming voice.

Abigail glanced at Mrs. Jessup, who was eyeing the young man with distaste. He was barely out of the schoolroom from what she could see. She glanced at her best friend, who was trying not to laugh and nodded once before looking away. "I would be delighted," she assured him, remembering her manners.

He smiled, showing off teeth that belonged in a horse's mouth. His delight was apparent to anyone who cared to look. "I will seek you out as soon as the music starts," he assured her. He bowed again to both her and Mel and forgot the older Mrs. Jessup, who harrumphed and mumbled something under her breath again.

"Why did you encourage me to dance with him?" Abigail asked Mel as they strolled along looking at people, nodding politely and being seen, an important part of these social gatherings.

"He was so earnest, and I thought you might enjoy dancing with him. It will give those," her head nodded back to the girls they had left, "something to talk about."

"They were nasty–" Abigail began, then put her hand to her mouth in shock that she had said it aloud.

Mel chuckled and nodded. "Your French is improving."

They enjoyed themselves. The young man's request for a dance was the first of many as gossip flowed that Abigail was the daughter of an earl. The gossip got a lot of facts wrong and frequently, Melissa Lawrence's name and value as an heiress was confused with her friend's background. Mrs. Jessup had a busy night keeping an eye on Abigail and the many young men who wanted to make the pretty young blonde's acquaintance.

Abigail was surprised when Victor Lawrence danced with her and asked if she was having a good time. Tongue-tied at the man's presence, she calmed when she realized how kind the man had been to her. After all, he valued her opinion on horses, and he was her good friend's father. She did wonder if he knew about Melissa's proclivities and if he approved.

Mel danced a few times, showing she was well versed in the current dances. Despite her height and girth, she was graceful, witty, and to some men's alarm, very direct. Older men appreciated her humor and honesty as well as her intelligence. One or two were looking for a second wife and considered courting the heiress. The young men, while trying to be polite, couldn't get past Mel's looks, and many times, she was taller than they. Her enormous wealth attracted only the ones that were down on their luck and looking to enrich their coffers.

Still, Mel enjoyed herself and was pleased to dance with her father on several occasions before the night was concluded.

"Did you girls have a good time?" Victor asked them both again at the end of the night as the carriage drove them back to their hotel. They would be moving on to other establishments in the next few days, having been invited to private homes for the rest of their stay before they would return to England.

Both girls assured him they had before fatigue quieted them and they were glad to go straight to bed. Mrs. Jessup was asleep almost instantly as she got into her bed next to her charge, and she never heard when Abigail got up to peek out the bedroom door.

Victor Lawrence had gone downstairs to smoke cigars with some men he had invited back to the hotel to talk business despite the lateness of the hour, and Melissa was alone in the living room. Abigail was about to go out to her when she heard a discreet tapping on the door to the suite and saw Melissa get up to answer it. She watched as Melissa snuck the seamstress into her bedroom, closing the door firmly, the sound of the lock distinct in the quiet of the suite.

Abigail returned to her bed, exhausted from the evening but thinking about everything she had observed. The American girl seemed not to care that the girls their age snubbed them, and the men their age were only after her money. She'd had lively conversations with older men, some who seemed interested in her, but Abigail wondered if they were just interested in the American's immense fortune. She had no idea how much money Melissa would one day inherit, but Victor Lawrence was not only generous with his only child but seemed to have no qualms about spending his money on his latest venture. Would he force Melissa to marry? Would she continue to seek out willing women? Why didn't Melissa see *her*? This, above all other things, was bothering the young woman.

Abigail brought herself back to the present, wondering if Melissa ever thought about her anymore in far-away Australia. What in the world could have she been thinking to stay there? How was it possible that she was married? She shook herself, knowing she needed to attend to people who would want to make their condolences directly to the widow of the earl. She must return downstairs; she'd spent enough time dreaming about another time and place.

She returned hours later after finding her ladies' study room in complete disarray. It was a room set off from the main salon where she attended her duties as chatelaine of the estate, and someone had rifled through the drawers and gone through the room quite thoroughly. The room was used for writing letters, and Augustus had finally told her not to bother sealing the letters as he wanted to read them before they were sent. It was on this edict that her letters to Melissa Lawrence had been snuck out of the house. He hadn't worried about any that arrived, just what she might be telling her mother, her sister, or her friends. He frequently corrected her spelling, or if her hand had been tired, he pointed out that she could have written it neater, sometimes even requesting that she rewrite something. She had resented this intrusion into something she considered private but had learned not to naysay him since it would lead to an argument. Whoever had gone through the room had done a thorough job of looking through things, not caring that someone would see the mess, and she spent time cleaning it up, nearly giving up the hour she had with her daughter to do so.

Spending time with Agatha had been rewarding even if the nursemaid was disapproving of any time that she spent with the child.

She liked to hear her daughter giggle when she played with her. She was so much fun, and Abigail only vaguely remembered her sister being this age since it had been so long ago. All too soon, her time with her daughter was cut off as she must be fed, bathed, and put to bed. She accepted the situation for now, hoping she would have the right to change it now that Augustus was gone. She headed for her own supper, finding a solitary meal not allowed even though visiting hours were long past. Her father was apparently staying in the house, having sent for her mother, her brother and his family, and her sister.

"Be sure to have the maids prepare rooms for them," he told his daughter, almost as though he had the right to order her about in her own home.

Abigail nodded, glancing at Mrs. Leister, who had overheard. The woman looked satisfied that a strong male was taking her in hand. She soon left the room as the two of them, at opposite ends of the long table, began to eat.

"Don't be silly, girl. Come down here and eat with me," her father ordered, gesturing from where he sat at the head of the table in Augustus' spot. Abigail realized her father was behaving as though he were lord of the manor and in the position of power. She tried to swallow her ire. He was usurping her husband's rightful place, appropriating it as his own.

"Thank you, Father. I prefer to eat alone tonight. I am in mourning," she reminded him in a sad voice.

"I can barely hear you. How are we to have a conversation if we have to shout?"

Since she had no desire to speak to him, she couldn't answer truthfully. "I appreciate your concern, Father, but I'd like to be alone with my thoughts."

"Nonsense! Move her place setting down here," he ordered one of the servants, and they obeyed him instantly.

Abigail found herself placed on her father's left side, resentfully sitting there as she looked down at the food they were served. Since her father was here, the servants were feeding them the preferred food instead of the secondary foods they would have given her if she had eaten in her rooms. She noted it included a nicer wine.

"I hope you will dress appropriately for Worthington's funeral," her father mentioned as he stuffed food in his mouth, not waiting for his mouth to be empty as he talked around the food, chewing with his mouth open. He eyed his daughter's dowdy gray gown distastefully.

Abigail tried not to look at her father; his eating habits had always disgusted her. She looked down at her food, eating it daintily as she swallowed before answering him. "Yes father. I have a dress that I will wear that is appropriate," she told him truthfully, not mentioning that it was being made especially for her. She remembered how he felt about new clothing, the expense not compatible with his thriftiness since he needed the funds for his own habits, which included gambling.

Abigail recalled when she and Melissa had returned to England. She had been so eager to share their adventures with the entire Baxter family while Melissa's father, Victor went off to inspect the work he was having done on the farms he had purchased.

"Oh, this is lovely, Abi," her younger sister enthused as she looked at the gown that Abigail had had made in Belgium. She was envious that her sister had gone to a grown-up party. She listened to the stories the two girls shared avidly, surprised that she was even interested.

"We've had several letters," Sir Anthony announced to his daughter a few days later, sounding aggrieved.

"Letters?" Abigail asked, surprised. Had someone reported her for inappropriate behavior? She hadn't done anything, had she? She quickly thought back to their trip and wondered if Mrs. Jessup had told him something. She immediately thought of Melissa's behavior and wondered if someone had seen something there. No, Melissa had been most discreet.

"Apparently, you made an impression in Belgium, and these are inquiries for your hand in marriage," he told her, looking thunderous. "I'll have no daughter of mine wasted on those Frenchies!"

"I think they are actually more Dutch," Lady Baxter tried to soothe him. She was just grateful he wasn't drunk for this conversation.

"Dutch, French, I don't care. I won't have it! My daughter will marry a good Englishman, or I'll know the reason why!" he thundered, pounding his fist in his hand and wincing at his own strength.

Abigail agreed, trying to reassure her father it hadn't been her idea, and she hadn't encouraged any of them. It took some convincing, with Melissa speaking up on her friend's behalf, before she was believed, but finally, he calmed down. Her brothers, Robert and Anthony, kept making faces behind their father's back, pleased that she had been called on the carpet for these unsolicited proposals. They couldn't believe that their little sister was of marriageable age and would tease her mercilessly when their father wasn't about.

"Can you believe that?" Abigail hissed once she and Melissa were alone.

"Actually, I can.   You looked very fetching," Mel told her, wondering why it was such an outrage to Sir Baxter that others would find his daughter appealing. "They obviously thought you worthy."

"But father was so angry," she said, sounding relieved to be away from it.

"Of course, he doesn't want to lose control of you to others.   It's ultimately his decision who you marry," Mel reminded her, suddenly feeling sad for her friend.   She knew her father wanted her to marry too but would never pick a husband for her.

Abigail resented that Sir Baxter had the final say of anyone she married.   He could force her to marry anyone he wanted to make a match with, and she wished it weren't so.   She glanced at Melissa and sat down on her bed.

Mel sat in the room's only chair and watched her friend, hoping she wasn't too upset.   She'd seen how Robert and Anthony had behaved. Not only had it been disrespectful to their father but also to Abigail.   If she hadn't wanted to marry Anthony before, she wanted to even less now.   What childish and inappropriate behavior.   She'd enjoyed some of the conversations she'd had on the continent with older men, finding men her own age more interested in what she could bring to a match or talking some drivel that only a girl with nothing in her head would be interested in.   The condescension they heaped on women set her teeth on edge.

"Oh, God.   Melissa, what will I do if he's horrible?" she asked, worrying about who her father would ultimately pick.

"Didn't your mother once say you weren't to marry until you were eighteen?" Mel asked, remembering something she had heard the older woman say.

"But I'll be eighteen next month. Didn't you know?" she asked, suddenly looking alarmed.

"Well, are you going to have a party?" she asked, trying to distract her from the thought of marrying someone she didn't want.

"No, Father says they are getting too expensive, and I have my coming out party next fall," she replied, sounding miserable.

"Well, we must have a private party then," Mel enthused to cheer her friend up.

"How can we do that? Father won't allow a party."

"Let's invite some of your friends," Mel began musingly. Even though she didn't like some of those girls, they *were* Abigail's friends. "We can have a picnic."

"Oh, you think we can?" The idea really appealed to her, effectively distracting her from her plight.

"Let's conspire with your mother. I'm sure she will say it's okay."

Completely distracted, Abigail was suddenly happy again as they made their plans. Melissa always made things right for her, and she didn't realize the affections she had for this American woman were turning from a juvenile crush into her first love.

"And you will have to give me those papers once you have signed them," her father returned her to the present with a bang, ruining the happy thoughts she had had over her first dress, the trip, and Melissa's promise to give her a birthday picnic. Apparently, her father had been expounding on some point to make himself heard in front of the servants and Abigail since they were his only audience.

Abigail suddenly realized her father had paused and was waiting for an answer. She swallowed the bit of crisp tart she had taken, nearly choking on the apple as it went down wrong. Using a sip of wine to help her, she heard her father continue.

"I hope you aren't becoming a drunk by drinking like that?" he had noted her hurrying to sip her wine, not realizing she had been choking.

"No, Father," she answered dutifully, annoyed as his own drinking seemed to be going on unabated. With Augustus' fine cellars, her father had several glasses with their dinner. She was just trying to get through this miserable dinner as he continued to abridge her for her behavior, berating her openly before the servants, expounding on how she should sign the papers and be done with it. The more he continued, the more she tuned him out, and she couldn't remember most of her dinner as she escaped into her memories. She finished up her dessert and waited until her father had a full mouth so he wasn't speaking before saying, "I have my duties to attend to, Father. If you will excuse me?" She got up and left the table before he could object, and she heard him coughing behind her, but she never turned, escaping out the door before he could call her back.

CHAPTER EIGHT

As she had planned, Abigail spent the night praying in front of her husband's coffin like a dutiful wife. She was wearing her gray dress, a scrap of lace placed chastely upon her hair as she bent her head. She had returned to her room after dinner to find it too had been thoroughly gone through, she supposed by her father. She didn't dare check the hiding place of the papers they were looking for, afraid someone would notice, and it would bring attention to their location. Instead, she used the necessary and then headed downstairs again to take up her station and start praying over Augustus. Naturally, after her initial prayers were done and the hours she knelt before the coffin dragged on, her mind began wandering.

She remembered her eighteenth birthday and how special Melissa Lawrence had made it for her. The Baxters couldn't have afforded the

fripperies, but Melissa had given her presents of the sort that made the day extra special for her, and she would always be grateful.

The day before the birthday picnic had been a blustery, late spring day. It was rainy and threatening to ruin the women's plans. Lady Baxter had been very accommodating to the idea of an innocent picnic for the girls. Mel had given Abigail a spring dress as a gift, and her father was willing to allow a seamstress to come in and make a dress for his oldest daughter as it didn't cost *him* anything. He thought it a gift from her American friend. This seamstress was nothing like the Belgian one, and Abigail was pleased to see that. Mel didn't even look at the woman twice. Instead, she was gazing at Abigail, as though seeing her for the first time as she stood there in her undergarments for her fittings.

"I do hope this rain blows away," Abigail fussed as the seamstress fitted her one last time, promising to have the dress done that evening.

"I'm sure tomorrow will be warm and cheery and all your friends will come," Mel reassured her, happy for her friend. She'd overhead Sir Baxter discussing who they might match his daughter with. He sounded very much like the horse breeders and owners she had overheard at the races they attended together. He had discussed the pedigrees and bloodlines of any potential suitors, and he had dismissed any of the foreign men who had sought his daughter's hand, even those who had determinedly written more than once. Instead, he was looking to find a man who could increase his own stature here in England through his daughter while she was still young enough to bear children. Mel had been nauseated as she contemplated her friend's fate. Over the months she had known Abigail, she had developed a real affection for this girl, who was now a woman. She realized there were deeper feelings there, but she had never acted on them and never even intimated that she was attracted to Abigail. She never would either. Abigail was clearly a friend, and she would do nothing to jeopardize that.

Abigail, however, had other ideas. She had carefully watched Melissa since their trip last spring after she knew she had been with that seamstress. She hadn't seen her with anyone else since, but that didn't mean Melissa didn't seek out others who might satisfy her needs the few times she wasn't staying with them. She felt strangely hurt that Melissa didn't see *her*. She was eighteen, quite grown up now, and she felt strangely drawn to Melissa. but she didn't know how to make her wishes known.

The next day, her birthday morning, dawned bright and beautiful. The storm had blown out to sea, leaving behind the promised warm temperatures, and it was cheery. Melissa had promised, and Abigail had gladly accepted, not only the gift of her beautiful day but also the dress that had been made especially for her. It was a light dress, gay and fun, and she could wear it all summer long. She looked pretty in the yellow material that was complemented with blue ribbons that showed off her pretty, blonde looks. Her other friends were thrilled to attend a picnic, and their beaus had been invited. A couple of her friends had tried to keep Mel from joining in, but Abigail wasn't having it. Mel was her special best friend, and she'd learned so much from the American. Just because she wasn't titled was no reason to snub her. Mel ignored them, used to these kinds of girls from her time at school and abroad. She'd learned long ago to avoid them, not respond to their taunts, and rise above them, which irritated them no end. She knew it was because they thought she felt superior to them and felt her money

made her better than them. That, added to the fact that she had no title, made her a non-entity to them. What they didn't know is that Mel had been hurt for so long by girls just like them that it no longer penetrated her thick hide. She was determined that this day, Abigail's eighteenth birthday, was going to be special. She had worked with Lady Baxter, who, despite her husband's edict, was going to make her oldest daughter's birthday special. The servants had been in on it, and the cook had even made a spun sugar cake, thrilled when Melissa had discreetly provided the funds necessary for the supplies. She was eager to show off her skills for the young lady. Abigail was well thought of in her father's household, and the servants wanted to see her happy.

The picnic was a delight, and the young women enjoyed themselves thoroughly in the warm sunshine. Those with beaus showed off a little, preening and posing with the young men. A few had brought brothers, who were hoping to catch the eye of some of the young women. Mrs. Jessup, Lady Baxter, a few well-chosen footmen, and Anthony and Robert Baxter were in attendance to make sure that no one went off by themselves.

Croquet and other amusements were set up on the lawns leading down to the river that flowed through the Baxter estate. Mel found herself sweating as she beat several of the young men, much to their disgruntlement.

"You should let them win," Anthony admonished, coming up behind her.

"Why?" Mel asked, looking at the young man in puzzlement.

The fact that he had to look up at the American woman annoyed the man. Just because of his sex, he felt he was superior to a mere woman. He hated that she towered over him, almost intimidating him. Still, she

was enormously wealthy, and for this reason, he could look past her many faults. As Robert had quipped, all pussies looked the same in the dark, and once he got several heirs from her body, he could ignore her and find a mistress that suited him. "You are hurting their feelings. They are my sister's guests," he told her haughtily, as though the American had no manners and should know better.

"What about *my* feelings?" she asked, looking sardonically at him. She knew he didn't like to argue with a woman, but she wasn't intimidated at all by him in all his maleness.

"*Your* feelings?" he repeated in astonishment. It had never occurred to him that she wouldn't bow to his wishes. She should let the others win. He had stated that, and she should do it.

"Yes, I have feelings too. Maybe they should step up their game and play better, so they could genuinely beat me," she pointed out. She had relished that last ball she had to hit, sending it sailing across the lawn and nearly into the river. The young gentlemen had taken several hits to get it back into play, losing horrendously to the rest of them. He had glared his discontent at the American. Mel wasn't doing anyone any favors.

He was astounded, intrigued, and more than ever, he was determined to bring this American woman to her knees. The thought of her on her knees before him had his member tingling, which surprised him since he felt she was so unattractive. He realized it was the power that was exciting him, not the ugly woman. He turned suddenly to hide his erection, shaking his head as he walked painfully away.

Mel didn't laugh aloud but she wanted to. She knew men didn't like to be shown up. Her father had explained it during the painful teen years when Mel had done that to others. It was a good thing she had left school and had a tutor, or she'd have embarrassed herself and any young man foolish enough to try and compete with her. Now, she shouldn't be so petty, and Anthony was right, she should let them win for their fragile egos. Still, it galled her to admit that.

"I hear you just won another round of croquet," Abigail said as she walked up, delighted for her friend. She couldn't hit the broad side of a fence with a ball and was terrible at sports. She linked her arm with Melissa's as she walked with her, drawing her away from the croquet, so others could play without the American beating them.

"Are you having a good time?" Mel asked her, enjoying the arm through her own as they strolled on the lawn.

"I am. This was a delightful idea, and Father certainly couldn't object, although I'm sure he tried," she muttered in an aside as she glanced at her beaming mother. Her mother and her best friend, Melissa, had made this happen. "Thank you for the idea of the picnic and thank you for this dress," she said, her hand brushing at an imaginary speck on the yellow linen.

"I'm so glad you like it," Mel told her, happy for her young friend and remembering her own eighteenth birthday. Her father had taken her down to Virginia to hunt on the farm they owned there. It had been delightful. She hadn't hunted here, although she heard they went to the hounds. Hunting a fox with hounds did not appeal to her or her father.

The day was declared a success as they ate along the river on blankets that the helpful servants laid out. Chicken and other cold foods were brought out for their guests to eat. Even though they were starving, the young women ate daintily and sparingly, so they didn't look like gluttons. They were jealous of the hungry, young men, who didn't have to be as polite. The men seemed to inhale the foods brought out for their enjoyment, even the wines and fruit juices. Lady Baxter had made sure none of their young visitors had more than one glass of wine, which they could ill afford, and this was used in a toast to her daughter on her eighteenth birthday.

All too soon, the afternoon waned, and the carriages and horses were brought to take their guests home before it got dark. A couple of the guests walked across the enormous fields to their own estates, escorted by servants, who had come to take them home and protect their charges. The day had been beautiful, and Abigail declared she would never forget it as she took off her birthday dress and changed into something more fitting for their dinner that evening.

Sir Baxter was at a race, which had allowed them to have the picnic without him in attendance. Everyone had been relieved not to have him there, unsure if he had even known about it or would have allowed it. Everyone in the Baxter household had wanted Abigail to have a nice birthday, so no one had told him. Her younger sister, Janie, had found herself falling in love with one of the young men who attended, following him all over the lawns until Lady Baxter had taken pity on him and called the young girl away.

Dinner that evening was formal, but the games they played afterwards—cards and charades—were just a nice family time together. There was none of the angst or anger that Sir Baxter brought with his demands and drinking. Even Anthony's imperious attitude when Melissa soundly beat him at cards was laughed off by Lady Baxter. She knew well the attitudes of this younger son of hers and thought he had no hope of convincing the woman or her father that he was a worthy suitor. The American was just so different from any other girl he had ever met, and her money was probably his only incentive. If he couldn't have the title, he would like to be richer than his brother.

Mel got ready for bed, pleased that the day had gone so well for her friend as she thought over the events of the delightful day. She knew her father would be coming to get her in a few days, and they would be traveling on to the south of England for more business investments. She'd be sorry to go, not having had a friend so close to her in a long time. She would miss Abigail and her family, despite Anthony's arrogant certainty that he could convince her father to let him have her hand in marriage. She started when the door opened, ready to admonish the servant who had come in without permission, and then stopped when she saw Abigail standing there in her robe, a candle on a candle holder held before her.

"Is everything okay?" Mel asked, concerned. She could see her friend's face in the light of the candle, and Abigail looked…worried.

"I just wanted to thank you again for making this the most perfect of days for me."

"You've already thanked me several times today for that very thing. You know you are very welcome," she replied, amused at the young woman's enthusiasm.

"I know, but I…" she suddenly lost her nerve, certain she had made a mistake as she leaned against the door she had come through, closing it behind her. She gathered her wits and would have left if Melissa hadn't spoken again.

"Was there something else?" she inquired, walking towards her. Abigail looked very fetching in the light of the candle, her light robe covering the nightgown she was wearing, her feet bare, and her hair released from its bun. She had brushed out the long tresses before coming through the door and it shone in the muted light of the candles.

Abigail looked at her friend, steeling herself. Without her normal day dress and wearing a dark robe that matched her dark hair, which she wore down, unbound, long, and luxurious, she looked...inviting, not intimidating at all. She had thought about this for a while, wondered at it, and now, she was here. She wanted this perfect day to end even more perfectly. "I was wondering...I mean...could you...would you...I...I..." she suddenly found her mouth too dry to speak.

"What is it, Abigail?" Mel didn't have a clue, and she was concerned that something might have happened in the few minutes it had taken for them both to dress for bed.

Suddenly, taking a deep breath, Abigail blurted out, "Would you give me a kiss, a proper birthday kiss?"

Surprised, it took Mel a moment to start smiling and nod. She leaned down and gave Abigail a kiss on her cheek, inhaling the scent of the blonde, who smelled of the violet water her maidservant bathed her in.

Exasperated, Abigail tried to turn in time to capture Melissa's lips, but the American's height put her lips immediately out of reach. "No, not like that," she said, putting up her hand to try to tug Melissa's head back down to hers.

Mel was puzzled. Abigail had never requested a kiss from her before. Of course, she had chastely hugged her friend from time to time, but now, she was confused by what the petite blonde wanted. She didn't dare to hope what it was Abigail really wanted. The thought didn't even enter the woman's mind that Abigail wanted more.

"Come down here," she whispered in exasperation, suddenly feeling as though she had a big letter A on her chest, and the servants would know why she was here in Melissa's room. She'd read that forbidden book over at a friend's house and thought the premise quite titillating.

Mel, still confused, bent down obediently and was completely taken by surprise when Abigail kissed her on the lips. She didn't know how to kiss properly though. Her lips were tightly shut, and she pecked at Melissa's lips, first one and then another, before pulling back and looking up at Mel as she slowly backed away in her confusion over the sudden attack. She brought her fingers up to her lips in wonder, looking down in Abigail's purple eyes. They were suddenly awash with tears, and Abigail turned to leave, feeling the rejection as Melissa stared at her in stunned disbelief.

"Wait! Don't go!" Mel ordered her, leaning against the door with her hand to prevent the other woman leaving.

"Don't...Let me go..." she said petulantly, feeling embarrassed. Melissa didn't want her. She didn't....

"Wait a minute," Mel soothed her, trying not to laugh in her own embarrassment. She was not sure if she should touch her friend or not. "What is this about?"

"Let me go!" she gasped, tugging at the door handle, trying not to let Melissa see her tears.

"No," Mel said succinctly, able to hear the tears in her friend's voice. "Tell me why you came here. Why did you try to kiss me?"

Keeping her back to Melissa, not looking at her directly or letting her see her mortification seemed to help. Abigail couldn't open the door without Melissa's cooperation because she was just too big and strong, and she didn't want to make a fuss. The servants or her mother

and brothers might hear, and she didn't want to alarm anyone that might still be up. This was all so embarrassing, not at all like she had fantasized. Melissa was supposed to wrap her strong arms around her, hold her, and return her kisses. She remembered how she had looked with the other woman. "I saw you in Belgium…" She gulped, trying to get the lump out of her throat. Maybe Melissa didn't want her. It had taken Abigail so long to work up her nerve, and she thought after the auspicious day they'd had maybe this was it…maybe this was the one chance she would have…. "I saw you with that seamstress…." she continued.

Mel was floored. She had been utterly discreet with the woman. Both women had enjoyed each other, but they knew it was fleeting, like enjoying another woman's body but no commitment and no messy emotions. Mel pulled away from the door, allowing Abigail to leave if she wanted. She walked backwards, away from the petite blonde, shocked that she knew. No one else had ever known…not her father and not his mistresses. Ever since New Orleans, when she had been taught by one of the best madams, she had been extremely discreet. Now, someone knew. Now, someone could expose her.

Abigail slowly turned, the tears drying as she saw the ashen look on the bigger woman's face. She hadn't expected that.

"Maybe you misunderstood…" Mel began, backing away from the blonde, ready with an excuse. She felt the bed behind her knees and sat with a thump, too shocked to react and knowing her excuse was feeble and a lie.

Abigail shook her head. They both knew it wasn't true. "I saw you kissing her in the shop. I saw her come to our suite at the hotel more than once."

Mel was astounded. That had been early spring and now, it was nearly summer, and her one true friend was revealing what she knew. Suddenly, she frowned as she thought about the matter at hand. "Why did you kiss me just now?"

Having the tides suddenly turned on her again, Abigail's breath caught in her throat. She thought of leaving. She had the means now but not the will. Her legs wouldn't let her leave. Her eyes bored into Mel's dark eyes, and she was trapped. "I wanted...I hoped..." she began, wringing her hands in her agitation. She was finally able to drop her eyes to the floor, which seemed to help make it less intense. "I wanted you to want me like that woman."

Mel was now speechless. She had never expected this. There was no way she could have predicted this. Yes, she had been attracted to Abigail for many months, but never—except in her wildest fantasies perhaps—had she thought that Abigail would want her too. She opened her mouth to speak, not once but twice. She looked like a fish gasping for air. Finally, the silence began to get to her. She could see that Abigail was about to run off, and she didn't want this between them. She didn't want to hurt her friend. Intending to let her down with a safe rebuff, the sensible thing to do in this situation, instead what came out was, "I do want you." She was just as shocked as Abigail at her words.

The blonde looked up again to see if Melissa was serious. She was stunned to hear the very words she had hoped to hear. "You...you do?" she stuttered.

Mel was having difficulty speaking. She nodded instead. Gulping loudly in the silent room, she squeaked out, "I never thought you would want this." She gestured at herself.

"I do," she answered fervently. Her legs still wouldn't work. They wouldn't propel her forward to Melissa, sitting on her bed in her nightgown and robe. Her legs wouldn't help her escape from the room or this uncomfortable situation either. "I've thought about it a lot since I saw the two of you."

"Why didn't you ever say anything before?"

"I was afraid."

"Not half as afraid as you are making me now," Mel mumbled earnestly.

Abigail heard her though and smiled for the first time in this uncomfortable meeting. "I've never seen you afraid," she stated, starting to feel a little braver. She had feeling in her right foot's big toe now. It was a tingling, so there was hope for her legs again.

"Geez, Abigail. You can't ever tell what you saw." She realized she sounded like she was back in the schoolroom and they were talking about tattling.

"I wouldn't," she said, shaking her head. There, her other toes were starting to feel the cold in the wood floor of the room. "I haven't said anything since I saw you two."

"Maybe you should have…to me."

They exchanged a look.

"What's it like?" Abigail asked.

"What's what like?"

"Being with a woman?"

"I don't know that it's any different from being with a man. I've never been with a man."

"Have you been with many women?"

"What kind of question is that?"

"Well, I think it's quite a practical question. If we are going to be together, shouldn't I know how many partners you have had?"

"What do you mean *if we are going to be together?* Who says we are going to be together?" Mel was feeling distinctly uncomfortable now.

"You don't want me?" Abigail asked boldly, her fears of rejection returning quickly. Her eyes widened, ready to start crying.

"Abigail," she entreated, wanting to rise and take the young woman in her arms. She just sat there instead. "You don't know what you are asking."

"I think I do," Abigail responded, suddenly looking older than her eighteen years. Mel felt trapped at that moment as she gazed in those beautiful, violet eyes.

"No, you don't want this life," she argued, trying to keep her head as she contemplated being with her friend, someone she had wanted for a while, but she was unwilling to lose a friendship over what she desired.

"What life?" Abigail asked, feeling able to walk forward and get closer to Mel. Tentatively, she sat on the edge of the bed but well enough away from Mel that she wasn't crowding her. Still, she was near enough if…. She wasn't sure what she wanted. Was it just to be held by this strong and capable woman, or did she want to be kissed passionately as she had seen her kiss the modiste? She'd thought about it often enough that she was certain she wanted the kiss…and maybe more. But what was more? She knew how horses did 'it.' She couldn't help but know that from being around the farms and studs and observing it, but as a well-brought-up Englishwoman, she pretended she didn't know how animals procreated. She'd seen dogs, ducks, and even one of the servants futtering another, but she wasn't sure how two women could do it, and she wanted to know so much more.

Mel sighed, knowing her blonde friend's curiosity might be her undoing, if she wasn't careful. She knew there was no hope for the two of them. She couldn't very well seduce an earl's daughter, who was destined for better things than an American woman could offer her, even a wealthy American woman. Abigail had to make an advantageous match, produce heirs, and be a dutiful wife. Indulging in a relationship with a commoner such as an American was thought to be wrong and would be frowned upon. Their friendship was only allowed because of her father's wealth. She understood that and accepted it, but she wanted more too. She had tried not to fantasize about it, but she couldn't help thinking that someday, she wanted a companion forever. Not a man but a woman that would be hers…until death doth part them. Dare she hope, even for a moment, that this young woman could be the one? No! She must not indulge her own fantasies this way. She had to set her friend straight. She began hesitatingly.

"A life of being alone for the most part," she told the wide-eyed blonde. "Finding others, who are interested in the same things you are," she gestured to herself, her body, and waited to make sure that Abigail understood before continuing, "…those who want to indulge in the pleasures of the female flesh."

Abigail desperately wanted the details. What pleasures of the flesh? She didn't dare ask but hoped Melissa would tell her, would provide those details.

"I don't think an Englishwoman such as yourself should indulge in such. You are expected to be a virgin on your wedding night for your

potential husband." *God, she sounded like such a ninny. Still, she must discourage Abigail.*

"What if I don't want my husband?"

She did have a point. "Didn't you once tell me that love wasn't for the members of *the ton*?"

"Yes, I've heard that you marry for wealth and status, and later, after the heirs are born, you can indulge in love with someone else." She said it prissily as though it were a fact and acceptable.

Mel felt sorry for her if she believed that. It sounded terrible to her. Then again, she didn't have many options. Yes, she could marry and have children with a man who would marry her for her wealth. He might possibly squander that wealth, but she would have status and position. He would receive an allowance, but the fact that he was her husband would allow others to let him borrow against his future allowance, and she would be expected to pay off his debts. She could still love women. No, she wouldn't do that to herself. She knew her father wouldn't let her marry a man that he didn't trust with his daughter or his money. It was one of the reasons she traveled with him and learned his businesses, so she had the knowledge to protect herself against such unscrupulous men. "Well, you aren't married, you aren't even engaged, and you shouldn't indulge with someone like me," she pointed out.

"Melissa," Abigail said quietly, her English accent weakening her and causing chills to run up Mel's spine at the sound of its soothing tones, "I've thought about you, about *this*, a lot since I realized what you were doing with that Belgian woman." She practically spat out the last two words, which left no doubt in either of their minds how she felt towards the woman. "I want to find out what it's like."

"No, Abigail. You are my best friend, and your parents trust me. If we indulge, they would never forgive me."

"They don't have to know," she said earnestly, sensing she was going to win this argument.

"What if they find out? There would be a scandal."

"They aren't going to find out. I certainly am not going to tell them," she said, sounding supercilious, something of the English aristocracy coming out in her tone.

Mel couldn't help but smile at the tone and her naivete. "But what if they do?" she asked, realistically.

"We will be discreet," she assured her, leaning closer and saying it softly.

"No, Abigail," she answered firmly. Abigail could be very persuasive, and Mel knew her own resistance was weakening. She sensed something she had always wanted but never dared hope to have was within her grasp. All she had to say was yes. She already knew her body was willing. The flesh was weak, but her mind told her to refuse this earnest, young woman.

"Yes, Melissa," Abi whispered as she came even closer, crawling up onto the bed in order to breathe it closer as she stalked the older and larger woman.

Mel leaned back, moving away from Abigail and nearly falling off the bed. She caught herself on the post and curtains and was trapped by them at the same time the blonde leaned in to kiss her again.

Abigail remembered the passionate kisses of the Belgian woman and how Mel had been so masterful. She realized her pecks hadn't been correct, and she leaned in, her lips lightly parted, not pulled into the bird-like peck she had been taught as a child. *Adults must kiss*

differently, she thought, and she put her lips against Mel's, hoping she was doing it right.

The relaxed feel of Abigail's luscious, little lips was Mel's undoing, and she couldn't help but respond. She also couldn't help but take control of the first real kiss they had ever shared. Her warm lips captured Abigail's, deepening it, teaching her as she pressed her own lips against the blonde's. Slowly, she opened her mouth. Abigail responded and did the same. As Mel expertly used her tongue, she was nearly undone by Abigail's copying of her ministrations. Her hands crept around the luscious, little blonde and began to caress her. Her heart melted further at the little moan she heard when she pulled Abigail on top of her and could feel her weight against her. Slowly, she stopped the kisses and pulled back. She had to try once more, at least for form's sake.

"Are you sure?" she asked the befuddled, petite blonde, looking anxiously into the glazed eyes for reassurance.

"Oh, yes, Melissa. Moooore," she breathed out enticingly.

Mel needed no further encouragement. She began to kiss her again in earnest, over and over. Slowly turning them, so they were side by side and her own weight was not imprisoning Abigail.

Shyly, Abigail began to copy the caresses, marveling at Melissa's size and strength and how much she wanted to feel her bare skin against her own. The muscles rippling under her fingers only invited her to caress and feel for more, to find out where this would lead.

Mel grasped the blonde's foot, caressing it and the leg attached to it, her lips applying feathery kisses about the ankle.

Abigail had never felt anything like that. It was as though butterflies were brushing against the skin of her ankle. Seeing

Melissa's bent head, she felt a warm rush of gratitude for her best friend's attentions.

Mel kissed her way up Abigail's body, her fingers caressing every inch of skin she bared to her touches. She looked up to see the eyes of her lover, dilated and trusting, wanting but not knowing what. She wanted to drown in those violet colors and kiss her senseless as she possessed this young woman.

Her senses had never expected to experience this overload. Abigail loved the feel of Mel's lips on her skin. Her fingers were delightful, but she wanted more, and she was anxious to experience everything.

Mel was in no hurry, delighting in the exploration of the young woman's body. She could already scent her arousal, wondering briefly if she was even aware of the copious amounts of fluid between her legs. She was obviously a true blonde, Mel noted in passing. She worked her way up Abigail's torso, avoiding the most sensitive area between her legs as she undressed her.

"Melissa...Melissa..." Abigail gasped as the brunette began to play with her nipples, which suddenly felt over-sensitized. She'd never thought someone kissing her nipples would feel so good.

Mel looked up, sharing a kiss with the woman and teaching her to open her mouth sensuously, gently touching the lips, the teeth, and her tongue to Abigail's. She could tell that she had never been properly kissed.

"What can I do for you? What do I do?" Abigail gasped when Melissa pulled back slightly, her hand enjoying the feel of the blonde's small breast in her palm. Her thumb and forefinger couldn't help but slightly squeeze at the erect nipple that begged to be suckled.

"You will want to do what I'm doing to you, but not right now…no, not right now," Mel told her. She wouldn't be able to hold back the passion that threatened to overwhelm her if this unschooled virgin even attempted to do these things. The intensity of her feelings would scare the young woman for sure. "I want to make love to you. I want to make it right for you this first time."

Abigail didn't mind. She was feeling a rush of gratitude for the way the woman was making her feel. She was being schooled and paying attention. She had no choice. Her body was very sensitized to Melissa's touch. It felt so warm and smooth, and she knew all the most pleasurable spots to touch the young woman.

Mel knew she couldn't give Abigail the ultimate kiss. She would be shocked, and she wanted this first time to be special for the woman. Instead, she finally allowed her fingers to play with the blonde curls between her legs, feeling the wetness as she tugged slightly on them before letting herself probe between the folds. She looked for and found the tiny nub that had the young woman gasping, not knowing it was even there. A finger curled inside, following the wetness. It was followed by another finger, widening the tight channel that had known no one…ever. Mel relished that she was Abigail's first and hoped that she would also be her last. She started to thrust, being careful not to go beyond a certain point, feeling the delicate bit of flesh that protected Abigail's virginity.

It was too much for the young woman. Having never had such stimulation before, she came before she could even understand the feelings that were building inside her. The tingling started, and she had no idea she was following a path that would lead to her destruction.

Mel captured her mouth just before she could shout out, having felt the copious cream on her palm and hearing her breathing change, rising with each gasp.

"Oh…OH!" Abigail's mouth was covered by Melissa's, and the echo of that last gasp was muffled.

Mel held her as her body convulsed slightly, pulling back her hand, so she wouldn't damage the tissue even as Abigail plunged her body and especially her pelvis almost violently against her in her passion.

A long time later, as Abigail came down from her first ever orgasm, Mel released her now cold lips and pulled her hand from where the blonde's legs held it tightly captive between them.

"That…was…marvelous," she said, wetting her lips with her tongue, surprised at how cold they felt.

Melissa smiled at her, pleased with herself and what she had accomplished. She desperately wanted to get off herself but didn't know if Abigail was ready to 'return the favor,' as it were. She wished they could have mutually caressed each other to fulfillment.

"Can I do that to you?" Abigail asked ingenuously.

"Oh, yes," Mel encouraged her, hoping she would. When she started, Mel helped her by showing what pleased and delighted her own overly sensitive body.

That night and many other nights when the American stayed with them, Abigail snuck into Melissa's bedroom, enjoying the education she was receiving from the older woman. She thought it a lark to sneak about, feeling there was nothing wrong with their love. If the servants noticed an increase in the amounts of body stains on the laundry, no one dared voice it.

When Melissa was gone with her father on their many trips, Abigail fretted that she would find someone else, someone more experienced. She delighted in welcoming her back, begging her mother to extend an invitation to that American who, although she was not of their class, had proven to be her best friend.

They made love mostly in Mel's guest bedroom but took picnics and daringly tried things out in the grassy glen as well as in the stables or anywhere else they could consummate their love. Both were young, carefree, and healthy, and their appetites for each other grew as they learned what pleased the other. It had been the best summer of Abigail's young life. Neither worried about how it would end, and once discovered, she had been quickly married off to Augustus.

Abigail looked up once again at the man whose body laid before her in the hall of their home. He had been kindly, if old-fashioned. He had protected her from her father. She hadn't missed that her father had checked on her a couple of times this night, to see if she was indeed kneeling there in prayer over Lord Worthington's dead body. She knew he was searching the house, trying to figure out where she had hidden the paperwork, so he could force her to sign it. She knew he could try and would keep trying. She hadn't caught everything he had said at the dinner table, too lost in her own thoughts and memories as an escape, but she had heard enough that in the past she would have capitulated to his bullying.

She felt herself wavering from the long night knelt in prayer. She nearly fell asleep near the dawn of another beautiful day. "Mr. Franklin, could you help me to rise?" she asked the butler when he came to check the hall early in the morning.

The man, much more respectful to her this morning after her vigil, offered his arm, but she was too weak from being in the same position for so many hours. It took the help of one of the footmen on the other side of her as her legs slowly regained feeling, and she stood there a while, trying to get her balance.

"I believe I will break my fast in my sitting room. Please have the cook send up a tray, and none of that food that Mrs. Leister has ordered be fed to me. I expect to be given the same food as my father or any other guest would receive," she told the surprised butler. "There will be no more of that behavior in this household, or I'll know the reason why," she warned him. She turned to the equally surprised footman, "If you would help me to my rooms?" She gestured to the steps where they were heading slowly. "And Mr. Franklin?" she stopped on the fourth step as the butler headed to the kitchens, "I do not wish to be disturbed, even by my father. I have done my duty to my lord," she gestured to her husband lying in state in the hall. "I will eat my breakfast in peace and catch some sleep."

The man nodded stiffly, not used to taking orders from the lady of the house. He responded to it as he had been trained to, but he realized that Mrs. Leister had ruled the roost for too long, and he had been derelict in his duties to his mistress. She was the chosen lady of the house. His master had never corrected their behaviors towards his young wife, and he would do well to immediately correct his own behavior. He exchanged a brief look with the footman who was helping her up the stairs on her unsteady legs and realized they were in complete agreement.

"Please have two guards placed outside my rooms in the hall. I do not wish to be disturbed once I have gone to sleep," Abigail told the footman after he helped her to the sitting room. She had to use the necessary badly but wouldn't have him take her there out of modesty. Her legs were still wobbly, but she would manage.

"Yes, my lady. Of course, my lady," he responded as was proper as he bowed his way out of the room. The look he had exchanged with Franklin told them both that this was a new order, and the mistress would be obeyed. He had heard Mrs. Leister complaining about some rudeness on the mistress' part, and he wondered if she had been told off. He hurried away to find two other footmen to guard the mistress' privacy. It wouldn't be easy as Lord Baxter had been on a tear. He'd talked to the maids, who had the duty of putting her room back in order after her father had gone through it looking for something.

Abigail hurried to her room to pull the chamber pot out and dropped her drawers, so she could use it. It was a relief to finally empty her overly-full bladder. She had been holding it in for hours and being pregnant, she found herself using the necessary much more often than usual, something she had noted when she was pregnant with Agatha too. She would have liked to have spent some time with her little girl that morning, but knew she had to get nourishment in her exhausted body and get some sleep. She was surprised that her rooms were quite in order after her father's attempt to find the paperwork. She thought briefly of going to get the papers and hiding them in here now that he had looked, but that was the exact kind of thinking that he would have too, and she knew he would come looking again. She hadn't had a moment to look them over other than a cursory glance, and she desperately wondered what they had to say. She would wait.

She was surprised and pleased to discover the cook had sent her food up so quickly when she walked back into her sitting room. The meal was pleasant and filling, and she found she didn't want the wine. She settled on some tea but would have preferred plain water. She left her dishes and headed for her bedroom, locking the doors as she got herself undressed and slipped between the covers. She wanted a bath desperately and determined she would have one once she awoke.

CHAPTER NINE

"You sent for me?" Mrs. Leister said frostily as she met Abigail in her sitting room. She didn't like that she had been *summoned*. She didn't like that the twit was sitting when she had to stand there waiting.

Abigail had just finished her bath and was now breaking her fast with toasted cheese and a glass of milk, which she had particularly asked for. She was pleased that her foods were to her liking, and she was no longer puking them up into the chamber pot. "I am *Lady* Worthington, and I would appreciate you respecting that," she told the prickly housekeeper from where she sat alone at her table.

The woman stiffened. She had been disrespectful to this girl since the day she arrived in her house, and it was a hard habit to break. "Of course, *my lady*," she said in a tone that sounded like she was having trouble to get out the words.

"I want the keys to the house. You've locked my husband's doors from me, and I want to know why?" she asked as she held out her hand for the circle of keys that were at the housekeeper's waistband, a sign of her importance in this household. Its removal would seriously hamper her status in the household as others would notice.

"The keys, my lady?" she asked, trying to delay the inevitable. She knew she really had no choice. If she was not to be dismissed, as she had been threatened before, she must obey the mistress of the house.

"Yes, give me your keys," she ordered, gesturing with her extended hand. "Is there a problem?"

"No, ma'am," the housekeeper responded as she reluctantly untied them from her waistband. She handed them slowly to the young woman, obviously unhappy with the task.

"Now, you will seek me out when you need to use them for the pantry and other rooms," Abigail told the woman as she dropped them in her lap and continued to eat. "You are dismissed," she said and saw the woman's expression. "I mean, you can return to your duties."

The woman left the room, seething at the impertinent young woman exercising her authority over her. If his lordship was still alive, she wouldn't have dared. She knew that the other servants would soon note she was missing her badge of authority, but she would show them. She would hold her head up, and she would soon have those keys back! Lord Baxter had assured her nothing would change, that she would still be in charge. She had helped him look for the papers he wanted, noting that the missus was rarely in more than a few rooms in this immense house and searching those rooms. She was much neater than Lord Baxter, who tossed not only the lady's office but her rooms, and he would toss them again. The housekeeper had searched the master's

rooms and found nothing out of the ordinary. She knew Lord Baxter was searching the little girl's rooms as she was outdoors with her nursemaid. She'd have to send maids to straighten it quickly, so her young ladyship was not disturbed by his mess.

Abigail felt the weight of those keys all through her breakfast. She allowed the maid to take the tray once she had eaten her fill. That too was a change as previously, Augustus and Mrs. Leister had determined how much she could eat at any one meal. The food had not only been of inferior quality at times, especially when Augustus was gone on his trips, but many times there hadn't been enough, even during her pregnancy. She looked down at the many keys on the ring, fingering them absentmindedly. She glanced at the door to her husband's sitting room and went to try them in the lock. It took some time, and she soon realized how many keys there were in this truly great house. Finally, she had that door open and found her husband's bedroom door between the two rooms was unlocked. So, the locking of the doors had been deliberate. She left the door wide open between both rooms and checked the door to the hallway. It was also locked, and she left that. She glanced towards the box in the closet that held the documents, tempted to fetch them and read them, but she didn't doubt that someone had told her father she was awake, and he would be looking for her and wanting to berate her. She couldn't be caught with the papers when he so desperately wanted her to sign them. She glanced around the room and noted it was cooler since there had been no fire in the rooms since yesterday. The air was much fresher for the windows having been opened, but someone had since closed them and pulled the drapes. She opened them, and that was when she realized someone had been searching in the room. Several things weren't as neat as they had been.

There were things ajar, not cleaned but moved from their usual place. Abigail desperately wanted to check and see if her paperwork was where she left it but didn't dare when she heard someone come to her sitting room.

"Ma'am? Lady Worthington?" a voice called. "Countess?"

Abigail walked quickly from Augustus' bedroom, leaving the door wide open. She swung by the door to the outer hall in his sitting room, making sure the door was locked. Anyone coming in here without a key would have to enter through her sitting room. "Yes, what is it?" she asked the maid who was looking for her and had gone into her bedroom.

"Ma'am," she said, curtsying. "Several callers are waiting to speak to you and pay their respects." She looked down at the floor, waiting for Abigail.

"Thank you. I'll be down shortly," she told the gal, who bobbed a curtsy and left the sitting room.

Abigail hurried to her room to primp for a moment, noting her room was back in order from yesterday and resenting that it had to come to this. She locked the door to her bedroom from the inside and then spent several minutes figuring out which key went in the lock of her sitting room, so no one could enter any of these apartments. Finally, she was able to go below to greet those who had come to express their condolences to the Lady of Worthington, because leaving just a card simply wouldn't do.

It was a long day and ended with the seamstress delivering her new, black gown. It was fabulous work, and they fitted her in her sitting room using a mirror brought from her room, which was full length and showed off the modern gown.

"This is lovely," Abigail said, trying not to preen. "Do you think it's acceptable to wear my mother-in-law's pearls to the funeral?"

"Oh, yes, ma'am. I've seen that many times. Pearls would be a nice contrast to the black of this gown and will look fetching across your bosom. It's a little tight here," she said, noting the waist was a bit snug.

"I've been eating too much lately with the worry," Abigail quickly distracted her as she took one last look and began to get herself out of the gown.

"You should have a lady's maid to help you, ma'am," the seamstress told her, helping with the last of the buttons.

"Of course," she agreed, but she had deliberately chosen not to have one more spy under Mrs. Leister's care in the time she had been at Hedgerows. She had told Augustus that it was to save on wages, which amused him as he could well afford a lady's maid. Still, he appreciated that she didn't spend money frivolously.

The dress was soon hanging in her dressing room, and she paid the woman on the spot, not waiting for the bill and instead using her accumulated monies she had saved from Augustus' monthly stipend for fripperies. Since she had never spent it, except to help her sister and Augustus had repaid her for that, she had plenty of money. The seamstress was astonished and pleased at the unexpected payment.

"Thank your people for their hard work and for finishing so quickly," she said kindly as she stood there in her dressing gown, wishing she could have worn the beautiful, if sad, black gown longer. Still, she would be wearing it all day tomorrow at the funeral.

"I will, ma'am. Thank you, my lady," the woman said, curtsying, her assistant helping her take the few remaining things they had

brought with them out of the room. They'd been prepared for anything in case her ladyship had wanted alterations, but she had been amazingly easy to work with.

Abigail closed and locked the sitting room door behind the woman and her assistant. She was finally alone and pleased for it. She had heard from one of the servants that her father had demanded the keys to her rooms. She'd ignored the demand as she was far too busy talking to those who came to pay their respects. Even dinner had consisted of her mother, her brother, Robert, Robert's wife, and her younger sister. Robert had pulled her aside after dinner and admonished her for not signing father's paper.

"It will help us out considerably. I don't know why you are constantly trying to thwart father's plans," he told her seriously.

It was then she realized that Robert had been convinced somehow that the Worthington estate was part of his inheritance. How dare they? How dare they assume they could appropriate her children's inheritance? She found herself avoiding him and his bride, a snooty-nosed woman, who constantly tried to look down on her husband's younger sister but had to curtsy to her since the Worthington name outclassed her own.

"I am sorry for your loss, Abigail," her mother tried consoling her when they had a moment alone. She looked at her daughter beseechingly, hoping she understood there wasn't anything she could do. Anthony was her husband, and she had to obey him. Good or bad, he oversaw their finances. She knew he desperately wanted to lay his hands on the Worthington estate, having speculated how much there was and how much it was worth.

"You know, I didn't love Augustus," she said quietly, looking at her mother.

"I know, poppet, but you did your duty and gave him a daughter."

Abigail wanted to confide in her mother but didn't dare. If her father suspected further secrets, he would bully the information out of her mother and try to manipulate Abigail further. She hoped she could bide her time until Mr. Adams returned. She didn't expect him for two more days and hoped in that time to find time to read her documents. She still had to check to see if they remained in Augustus' dressing room. She'd been on pins and needles since she realized someone had been through his things.

Finally, she was alone. Locking the door, she took a lamp into Augustus' sitting room and walked through the fine furniture and towards his bedroom. She could see no one had been in these rooms since she'd locked the doors and confiscated the keys. She put the lamp down on his dresser and went immediately to the box where she had hidden the papers. Reaching inside, she didn't find them, and her heart immediately jumped into her throat. That meant when Mr. Davis and whoever came to help her asked to see them, they would be delayed and refused, and her husband's solicitors and her father would try to manipulate her in some way. As her father, many people would assume he was acting on her behalf and would do anything he told them. Already, she had seen the way the servants deferred to him and his orders. She couldn't allow that. Reaching in farther, she felt the parchment and tilted the box towards the light. They were there but had fallen against things that were stored in the box. She sighed with relief, quickly putting things back and closing the box, then returning it to exactly where it had been in the room. She hastily took the lamp and

went through her husband's sitting room to her own. One by one, she put the lights out herself, knowing this was a servant's job but preferring to be alone and do it herself. She left one light on in her room as she got ready for bed. She was exhausted from all the social niceties she had to conduct that day. She knew the funeral the following day would be tedious, and she knew once it was over, her father would insist that she stop this foolish nonsense and sign the damn papers.

CHAPTER TEN

Abigail remembered when her father had discovered her and Melissa in bed together, naked. It had been horrifying. Melissa had tried to shield her body from her father's view. He had been furious. She had known he had been suspicious, having checked on her many times, once, appearing unexpectedly in her room and opening the door, hoping to catch her at something. She had been reading a book that time and had jumped up in alarm at the door slamming open.

"Father?" she asked, surprised at the invasion of her privacy. She pulled her covers up above the nightgown she was wearing and glanced at her mother, who gave her a warning shake of her head.

"What's this I hear you ain't sleepin' in yer bed?" he asked, looking around the room curiously, hoping to see some sign of someone or something that would tell him what was going on.

"But I am," she said sensibly, gesturing at her bed. She tried to look confused, but her heart was beating hard. Melissa wasn't even in their house; she was off on one of her father's many business trips.

"Well, see you keep it that way," he said gruffly, seeing nothing was amiss and feeling embarrassed for the display.

A week or so later, he had caught her in Melissa Lawrence's bed, and her world had changed forever.

"What in the name of all that is holy is this?" he roared, startling them all.

Mel had rolled Abigail to the side, trying to shield her naked body from her father's view and covering them both with the bedclothes.

"Fa...Father!" Abigail gasped, shocked to see him coming through the door.

"What the hell do you think you are doing?" he yelled at her. Her mother's face appeared over her father's shoulder, seeing Melissa and Abigail in bed, both obviously naked. Her eyes widened at the sight and its implications.

Neither young woman knew what to say as they stared at the adults, who stared back at them in shocked horror.

"Get your clothes on," Lord Baxter ordered his daughter ominously.

"Y...Yes, Father," she answered meekly, but as she went to get out from under the covers, she realized her state of undress and stared, unwilling or unable to move.

"Well, girl? What's keeping you?" he snapped, not understanding.

"Anthony, you need to come away," Lady Baxter tried, taking pity on their oldest daughter.

"I will not! This is my house and finding this going on under my roof is unacceptable." He looked apoplectic.

"She cannot get dressed until you leave," she said reasonably, glancing warningly at the young women to say nothing as she tried to distract him.

Lord Anthony Baxter blinked, glanced back at the two young women holding the bed clothes up to their chests with their hair in disarray, and swallowed. He was very aware of what he had interrupted, and he would never be able to forget the sight of his daughter and that woman; it was burned into his mind. Turning, he faced his wife, then glanced down the hall where his other children had popped out of their rooms at the commotion. "Get back to your rooms!" he ordered, turning his anger on them. Seeing he had obviously alarmed the servants with his raised voice, he turned it on them as well, "Don't you have something to do?"

"Girls get yourselves dressed," Lady Baxter told them warningly as she gave her husband a slight push out the door and closed it.

Abigail had put on her nightgown and wrapped her robe around herself. Seeing Melissa dressing she hissed, "Are you leaving?"

"I should, shouldn't I?"

"I don't know," she admitted, biting her lip endearingly. She was very afraid of what her father would do. Melissa had warned her about being caught. She'd waited until she was certain everyone was in their rooms for the night before sneaking down to Melissa's room. She had grown complacent with their regular lovemaking throughout the summer, and she'd forgotten about the others in her life and her coming out party that was scheduled for this fall.

"Are you decent?" her father's voice came through the door far too soon.

Melissa nodded at her friend, ripping a stocking as she pulled and adjusted it, wanting to cry over the tear and at the same time just wanting to be finished dressing.

"Just a moment, Father." Handing Melissa her top, she helped to tie the ribbons that held it together, brushing at the exposed skin before the petticoat ties hid it. She hadn't meant for that to happen, but she handed Melissa her skirt before turning away and heading for the door. Opening it, she saw both her parents waiting.

"Go to your room, Abigail," Lord Baxter ordered.

"Father, I can–" she began, not knowing what she could really say.

"Go to your room, miss!"

Frightened, Abigail glanced at her mother, who was looking down at the floor, ashamed as she rushed by her.

She had thought never to see Melissa again, but several weeks later when going to the stables for her customary early morning ride, she was startled and nearly screamed when a hand reached out and pulled her into a vacant stall. The hand covered her mouth, silencing her, and was held there as the young woman's eyes adjusted to the gloom. Her eyes widened when they adjusted, and she recognized the much bigger Melissa Lawrence. She had thought from the person's size that it was a man. Slowly, Mel released her grip as Abigail calmed, her own hand going to her mouth in a gesture of silence as the brunette's fingers pressed against her lips

"What in the world?" Abigail gasped when she was released, whispering it loudly but earnestly. "Do you know what my father would do if he discovered you here?" She knew. It had been made very clear to her that the American would die a horrible death if she were caught anywhere near the earl's daughter. Only the fact that

Victor Lawrence was so well known, had very important ties, and had the money to back up anything he wanted to do, kept the earl from exacting revenge. Lawrence's daughter could stay the hell away from his daughter! He only hoped he could marry her off before the gossip reached the wrong ears. He knew the servants couldn't help spreading gossip.

Mel nodded. "What is this I hear about you marrying Lord Worthington?" she asked, the knife in her heart turning slightly and gutting her.

"My father says I have no choice. No decent man would have me if they found out about my..." she looked down as she sobbed slightly, "my proclivities. I think my mother convinced him it was you who led me astray." They both knew the lie to that statement, but Abigail hadn't been asked, and she certainly wouldn't volunteer the information. She looked back up at the angry American.

"How can you?" she asked.

"You don't understand. Lord Worthington will be paying off my father's debts, and we won't be losing our home," she sobbed slightly as she looked at her, trying to make her understand. She had to make this sacrifice for her mother, her sister, and her brothers. That had been made very clear to her once they knew what she had been up to. The humiliation had been brutal. She had been given no choice. Either she married this man and soon, or they would turn her out. The alternative was a convent or an asylum, and she'd overheard her mother arguing furiously with her father about *that*. She must be weak in the head to prefer women over men and have *unnatural* inclinations such as this.

"So, you will give yourself to this man for your family and for your father's gambling habits?" Mel asked, incredulous. "I want you to

come away with me. I have more money than they, and we can live quite–"

"You don't understand, Melissa. My family would be destitute. We would lose all this." Her gesture took in the stable and everything beyond it including the lush lawns leading up to the great house. "I can't do that to my family. I owe them."

"I could pay off–" she began but saw the horror on the young woman's face at the suggestion. She imagined speaking to the earl about his debts and dismissed the thought. She changed her tactics. "What do you owe yourself? What about us? I love you, Abigail," she told her earnestly, her young heart trying to pour her emotions into her few words.

"I'm sorry, Melissa. What we had was an aberration. It's not normal. I can't–" she broke off as she attempted to leave the stall. "I'm sorry, Melissa," she repeated as she looked in the taller woman's eyes to try and make her understand the sacrifice she was making. She briefly considered kissing her goodbye but knowing that it would be their last kiss, she couldn't trust herself to let her go. She knew what would happen in this lonely stall with no one around to stop them. If her father found out, he would kill Melissa, and Abigail would either go to an asylum, a convent, or be thrown out, never to be spoken of again.

"No! Don't go!" Melissa pleaded, but the smaller blonde slipped out and didn't look back, leaving her heartbroken as she realized what she had lost.

Two weeks later, the banns had been read. No gossip about anything the young girl might have done would be believed. She had made an advantageous match for her family. Her father and his

finances were solvent, and she would breed Worthington a slew of sons for his many estates. A few mentioned that now, she wouldn't need the coming out party that had been planned for that fall; a couple making snide comments about how it had saved her father the expense of such an extravagance.

Abigail thought of inviting the Lawrences to the wedding but knew it wouldn't be allowed. Then, she heard that Victor Lawrence had suffered a fatal heart seizure and died. She had wanted to go to Melissa, but she was already carrying Augustus' first child and was being watched carefully. When she heard that Melissa had begun to sell off the farms and horses her father had so carefully purchased, it had been her suggestion that Augustus check out these 'deals' and see if he could improve his stud. He had grasped on the idea, patting his young bride on her head for the idea he took as his own. He had thought he profited greatly by the sell off, never realizing how much Melissa Lawrence had made on the deals.

As her memories assailed her, Abigail realized she had to get up. The funeral was today, and she needed to break her fast. She wished she had someone to lean on, but Melissa had been her only true friend, and she had hurt her so terribly. At that moment, a plan began to form. It would all depend if Mr. Adams could pull off what she hoped would be a coup from her father and her husband's solicitors. She rang for a maid, unlocking her door and ordering a tray to be brought to her.

"Your father insists that you eat with the family, ma'am," the maid apologized, curtsying.

"Oh, he does, does he?" she murmured, already annoyed at her father's high-handedness. Maybe she should take a few leaves out of Melissa Lawrence's book. "Help me dress," she ordered the maid.

She was dressed in the elegant black dress in no time, her hair brushed out and put up as a woman of her station warranted. She looked in the full-length mirror, pleased with what she saw. She was young, but she looked properly gowned for the first time in a long time. Not since the gown she had had made for her at Melissa Lawrence's expense for her birthday had she owned a gown that not only fit her but conformed to society's norms. As she put on the pearls and attached the earrings, the first she had ever owned, she thought about how she would treat her family, especially her father. The nervous flutterings in her stomach had nothing to do with the baby. She only hoped she wouldn't be sick that morning as she strode down the hall to the steps.

She glanced at Augustus lying in state in the hallway and was glad that he would be buried that day. If he lay here any longer, he would begin to stink. Entering the breakfast room, she was annoyed to see her father holding court at the head of her table, almost as though it were his right. "Good morning," she stated in reply to her family's greetings. She could see her father staring suspiciously at the gown she was wearing. Her mother and sister were admiring the gown, but her brother didn't notice as he concentrated on his food, and her sister-in-law just glared.

"Eating light?" her mother inquired gently, seeing the foods that Abigail chose from the buffet.

Abigail had noticed that the food was all nicely displayed, and she couldn't fault the servants for showing off her silverware and the many selections.

She sat as far away from her father as she could, since her mother was on his one side and her brother on the other. Carefully, she covered her gown, so she couldn't get food on it. She wasn't going to ruin how good she felt in the gown by spilling something on it. "Yes, I thought today would be trying," she answered somberly, trying not to look at her father, who was slurping something.

"Yes, it will be a long day," her mother replied, sipping delicately at whatever was in the glass she held.

Abigail tried not to speak, wanting to get through this meal without the anger she felt at her father's presumptuousness.

"Have you signed those papers?" her father brought up when he had finished the mound of food before him. It was his third helping, and he had not deigned to help himself from the buffet but had demanded a servant serve him.

Abigail closed her eyes briefly, praying for patience. "No, Father, I haven't," she answered tiredly. She hoped she wouldn't get indigestion and further prayed that no morning sickness would afflict her. The seamstress had insisted on a tight corset, and she'd kept the laces loose, especially around her stomach. The maid had been inexperienced and hadn't realized they should be tight, cutting off her breath.

"Why not?" he asked, sounding perturbed.

"I haven't had a chance to read them yet," she answered honestly, hoping to avoid an argument.

"Read them? You don't need to read them. Just sign them already!" he demanded, his fist crashing down on the table and causing several people to jump.

She didn't answer, realizing that whether she did or not wouldn't change his irritation with her. She calmly finished her toast, the eggs suddenly seeming unappetizing and the rashers of pork too greasy. She heard people arriving in the front hall and Mr. Franklin answering the summons at the front door.

"Lady Worthington," he said pompously at the door to the dining room where they were all eating, or in her father's case, glaring at his daughter. "You have visitors that demand your attention."

Abigail looked up, pleased for the interruption.

"They can just damn well leave their calling cards and go," Anthony Baxter told the butler.

"I'll be right there, Mr. Franklin," she told the butler kindly, wiping her lips delicately with her cloth napkin.

"You haven't finished your breakfast," her mother reminded her gently, something that wouldn't have been allowed at Baxter Hall.

"I know, Mother, but it can go to feed the pigs," she said kindly in return as she rose from the table.

"I haven't excused you, miss," her father's voice stopped her for a moment.

Abigail turned and looked her father in the eye. "I do not need to be *excused* from my *own* table." Her heart was beating hard in her chest, and she turned around as the gasps rose from the table, and she left the room. She could hear her father sputtering behind her and her mother's soothing tones as she followed Mr. Franklin towards one of the sitting rooms.

"Lady Worthington," Mr. Adams greeted her, taking her hand and kissing the back as he bowed. "Let me introduce my colleagues to you," he said kindly. "This is Mr. Cherwin, Mr. Elmswood, and Sir Boardman. They rode hard to make this meeting for you," he informed her meaningfully.

Abigail wasn't sure of the social protocols, but she curtsied to each of the men as they were introduced and they bowed, raising her eyebrow at the introduction to Sir Boardman. "*Sir* Boardman? Are you a solicitor then?"

"I am, my lady. I know it is unusual for the gentry to be involved in business or the law, but I could not help myself," he told her charmingly, raising her hand and kissing the back gallantly. His blue-green eyes sparkled as she looked in his eyes with her amazing violet-colored ones. "I am a second son, and as I wouldn't inherit my father's titles, I went into law."

"Please, be seated," she offered them all, not in the least intimidated by the men whose friendly smiles encouraged her.

"Did you manage to obtain the paperwork?" Mr. Adams asked her, an anxious note in his voice.

"Yes, and my father has been scouring the house looking to find where I hid it all. He demands that I sign the papers he had drawn up, and I have put him off with my duties for my husband's funeral."

"I am sorry that we came at such a stressful time for you, my lady. Perhaps, we should come back?" Sir Boardman asked, looking anxious.

"No, I would like for Mr. Adams to read through the papers. I haven't had a chance with them watching me constantly."

"Watching you, madam?"

Not wishing to sound disloyal to anyone but at the same time wanting them to realize her predicament, she explained, "This is my husband's home. I have never been more than his wife and have had no other duties than to produce heirs for him. The servants are loyal to him, not me. My father has assumed his place."

"Usurped is more like it," Sir Boardman replied, his eyes twinkling at hers when she looked up in surprise. "I am sorry, my lady. Perhaps, you would prefer I be respectful? I know who your father is."

"No, I'm very well aware of who and what my father is, but who are you?"

"Ah, I should have explained," Mr. Adams interjected, trying to keep things light. He didn't want to intimidate the young woman as she had trusted him. "Mr. Cherwin and Elmswood are both men of business, but Sir Boardman is with the London bar and even works with parliament occasionally."

"You downplay my role," Sir Boardman sounded wounded as he smiled in delight. "I'm a bit of a back-room player, madam, if you need such a person on your side."

"If Mr. Adams trusts you, then I will trust you. My good friend, Melissa Lawrence, trusts him, and I must also. I cannot sign those papers without solid advice. My gut tells me it is not to my benefit."

"Never sign papers blindly," Sir Boardman quipped. "We must read those papers and come up with a plan for you."

"I did manage to get a copy of the will," she told them and was pleased to see how happy that made them. "I will go and fetch everything. Have any of you eaten?"

"No, ma'am. We came here directly from Adam's home once we caught some sleep," Mr. Cherwin put in, and the other men nodded.

"I would rather you didn't interact with my father. He has a way of worming out information, and until we know what we are dealing with, I would rather he remain ignorant. He assumes too much," she said, feeling morning sickness rising in her belly as she thought about her father and the fact that she just might thwart him and his plans. "My brother, Robert, is here too, and he is trying to get me to do my father's bidding."

"Do not sign anything, my lady," Mr. Adams advised her. "Until you have a clear picture of what your husband left you and what your children, er child has inherited, we need to act carefully."

She exchanged a look with him, not wishing to draw attention to the child she was carrying. "I'll fetch the paperwork," she said, rising.

All four men rose with her, bowing slightly as she curtsied and hurried to the door. She was just in time to catch Mr. Franklin hurrying from the doors. "Mr. Franklin," she called, and he turned around, his face appearing innocent. She gestured to bring him closer. "Is my family done eating? Have the servants cleared the breakfast?"

"Yes, ma'am. Your family are walking in the gardens; your mother felt your father could use the air before the funeral. The servants have begun to clear–"

"Tell them to wait and escort these gentlemen to the breakfast buffet. Have places made at the table for them, so they may eat." As Mr. Franklin went to do her bidding, she stopped him. "Mr. Franklin, I do not appreciate being eavesdropped on, and if my father should get word of who those men are or what you have heard, you will be forced to find yourself another position."

Having already turned away, the butler swung around in surprise, looking down on the petite woman. "Ma'am?" he questioned, trying to sound as though he didn't know what she was talking about.

"You heard me. Things have been not to my liking for a long time, and with my husband's death, they are going to change. If you don't like your position, I will understand, and I will accept your resignation, but if you wish to remain, then things will be different. Do I make myself understood?"

"Impeccably, my lady," he said, bowing.

"Then, you may go," she said, watching as he hurried away. Her heart was going to pound out of her chest this day, and she glanced at the dead man in her hall, blessing him for having died and giving her the strength she might need to get through this day. She hurried up the stairs to her room, unlocking the door quickly now that she was more familiar with the keys. She found her room in disarray after having been rifled again. Her sitting room wasn't as bad, but it too had been gone through again. She wondered how they had gotten in and hurried to the other door. She unlocked the door to her husband's sitting room and found it in the same condition it had been before, hurrying through it to his bedroom. She was relieved to find the box in his dressing room. Taking it down and opening it, she reached in for the papers, making sure that they were all in her hand, then rolled them up and closed the box, putting it back in the exact spot where it had been. She unlocked the door to the hallway and made her way back to the stairs. Seeing a maid, she ordered, "I want my bedroom and sitting room straightened up. Whoever went through it is about to lose their position, if I find out who it is. Do I make myself clear?"

The startled maid nodded and shook her head as she realized the precarious position she might be in. Mrs. Leister had ordered her to look for some paperwork for Sir Baxter, and she now saw a roll of parchment in Lady Worthington's hand, which might be what they had been searching so diligently for. "Yes, ma'am. Right away, ma'am," she said, curtseying and hurrying to get away and do her bidding. She had only been following orders.

Abigail found the men enjoying their breakfast. Some of the food had been taken back to the kitchens for reheating, but they could enjoy it once again when it was returned to them. They appreciated Lady Worthington's care for their nourishment.

"Is that all of it?" Mr. Adams eyed the rolled-up parchments Abigail was carrying.

"It is. I had it hidden," she admitted, handing it to the man and wishing she had read it all.

"We'll look everything over," he said, putting the roll in his jacket pocket and digging into the plate a servant had brought him from the kitchen. It was hot and smelled delicious.

Abigail put her hand to her stomach, the smells not to her liking. "Gentlemen, if you will retire to the sitting room after your meal, so you can read through the paperwork, I will ensure no one will disturb you. I must attend to my duties."

"Thank you, Lady Worthington," Mr. Adams answered for them all as she rushed from the room, trying not to let anyone see her sick.

"How old is that young woman?" Sir Boardman asked Adams around a mouth full of bacon.

Adams looked up from his fine meal. He didn't want to talk, he just wanted to eat. They had all gotten up early after arriving so late at his home, and he hadn't had a chance to eat a good meal. This looked good, tasted great, and he wanted to eat it uninterrupted. "I believe she is twenty-one."

Sir Boardman looked thoughtful as he picked up his toast to eat.

They all ate well, and when they were finished, they went back across the hall to the sitting room, closing the door behind them and locking it as they began to go over the paperwork Lady Worthington had provided. They could hear the noise of the people who were arriving and taking the now closed coffin to the small church on the

estate before it would be taken to the newly dug grave. It would be many hours before anyone would bother them.

CHAPTER ELEVEN

Abigail did her duty. She followed Augustus' coffin as the men bore it to the church and then to the grave, holding her young daughter's hand and lifting her when she tired. She listened as the elderly man sermonized over her husband; he had known Augustus all his life. It was long, hot, and boring. She kept her face carefully schooled in a solemn mask of mourning. She accepted the condolences of people both titled and common. She was surprised at how many people had attended but then saw that those who were titled were there only to be seen, and those who were untitled were there because he had been their landlord. She wondered if they would have come otherwise.

Several times, her father had attempted to talk to her again. He had thought over her impertinence and was wanting to reprimand her for it. Her mother had distracted him admirably time and again, and of course,

as the widow of the Earl of Worthington and his countess, her time was taken up by the various people that had attended the service. It wasn't until late in the afternoon that she managed to knock on the sitting room door and see the four men, who had been going over the paperwork since that morning. She was pleased to see they had refreshments. Someone on her staff was making sure they had been taken care of.

"Gentlemen," she said in greeting as she slipped in the room, closing the door firmly behind her and hoping no one had seen where she had gone.

"Lady Worthington." They all rose and bowed to her. "Countess," Sir Boardman greeted her.

"Please, be seated," she told them as she hurried to sit on an empty settee across from them.

"If you don't mind, madam, I have sat more than enough today and would prefer to stand," Sir Boardman informed her, and at her nod, he stood again.

"Lady Worthington, we would advise you not to sign these papers. It essentially gives your father full control over your finances as well as your daughter's inheritance. In the event of your father's demise, control is then given outright to your brother, Robert."

The feeling in Abigail's stomach confirmed what she had suspected. She nodded; her purple eyes wide as she listened. The men took turns pointing out the various properties that she now owned that were left to her as the earl's wife and were to be held by her for her children. She was surprised how much there was. She had known about the farms and the mills but had not realized how many there were or how extensive until the men explained.

"Your father isn't in any hurry to turn over the title to the new earl either," Sir Boardman mentioned when he had a moment. "I can see here that the new earl isn't guaranteed the monies from the estate, only the title. He isn't even allowed to live here at Hedgerows unless you find it amenable."

"My husband worded his will like that?" she gestured to the paperwork they had been pouring over for hours. She hadn't thought he had any faith in her.

"No," Mr. Adams told her, looking at her intensely. "He left it so that whoever executed his will would be administering it for you. He felt you were too young and too flighty, but he wanted his heirs taken care of, and they would have the funds when they reached their majority. It doesn't say that you must use your husband's solicitors either. You can appoint anyone you wish," he pointed out.

"It says that?"

"No, it does not; however, the laws of England will allow you to appoint other caretakers, so the extensive properties your husband inherited and accumulated in his life can be managed for you," Sir Boardman interjected.

"Lady Worthington, I don't think you want the responsibilities of running a mill by yourself, am I correct?" Mr. Cherwin asked her.

"No, I do not think I am in the least bit inclined to do so," she answered with a self-deprecating little smile that they responded to.

"Then let us manage this all for you," the man said, his hand taking in the paperwork. "Do not sign away your rights with this," he indicated the papers her father had wanted her to sign. "I know mills, which is why Adams here sent for me."

"And I know horses," Mr. Elmswood put in. "Which is why I was sent for, right Adams?"

Mr. Adams nodded.

"And I know the law, and the men who drew up your husband's will assumed they'd be administering it for you. They thought you were a simple miss, who would go along with your husband's wishes. They probably didn't anticipate Sir Baxter entering the mix, and he probably bullied his way until they agreed to him administering the estate with them. They don't realize how incompetent he is."

At the word 'incompetent' she looked up, wanting to defend her father and his name.

"You know your father has been close to bankruptcy several times in the past?"

She hadn't known, but she suspected, especially with all the loans her husband had made him over the years.

"Your father is an inveterate gambler, and he hasn't been winning, despite his boasts and appearances to the contrary. All your father's debts to the estate were forgiven upon your husband's demise."

She hadn't known that either. She knew he couldn't afford to ever repay them, but hearing it stated so blatantly, she was ashamed. "What about my mother, my brother, and my sister?" She wouldn't mention her other brother. He had written her off years ago after what he had said upon finding out she had loved a woman, and she didn't think of him.

"That is not your concern. I understand that you made it possible for your sister's wedding to take place. You are not obligated to her in any way. What your father leaves your brother is whatever he hasn't gambled away. As to your mother, you can offer her a place in your home when your father is destitute, and from what I have seen that may be in the very near future."

She was feeling very hot and embarrassed because of her father.

"I'm sorry, Lady Worthington, but your father has nothing to do with Lord Worthington's estate unless you allow him. Do not sign this," he indicated the papers. "It puts you in an untenable position. I wouldn't be surprised if the new earl could be bribed by your father into doing whatever he wants regarding the estate, even if he doesn't have the means, he would certainly have the power as the new earl."

She looked up at this and glanced at Mr. Adams, who shook his head slightly, indicating he hadn't told them about the baby. She raised an eyebrow and then glanced at the other men meaningfully. Mr. Adams nodded discreetly. She could tell them. "Sir Boardman, I have no intention of signing those papers." She saw all the men looked relieved at this statement. "I too believe Mr. Adams brought you all here for your expertise. I trust you because I trust Mr. Adams. I trust Mr. Adams because my good friend, Melissa Lawrence, trusts him. I hope that trust is never found to be misplaced." She waited a second as they all nodded, reassuring her. "As to the new earl, we won't know about that for another six months." She raised her hand as Sir Boardman made to interject. "Mr. Adams knows, and I appreciate the discretion, but I am enceinte, and the earl knew this before he died. As we won't know the sex of the baby until then, it can't be decided who the new earl is. If it isn't my son, then I don't want him living here having anything but the title."

"Your father will try to–" began Sir Boardman again.

"My father won't be able to find me," she interrupted. "If I'm not mistaken, my husband owned a house in London. I will go there with

my daughter and will take none of the servants from here at Hedgerows. None of the servants here are loyal to me. I want the staff cut to the bare minimum, just enough to maintain this beautiful estate for my heirs." She dramatically caressed her stomach, the bulge not noticeable until she pulled on the fabric. "If my father can't find me, he can't bully me into anything. My mother can contact me through all of you, but I do not want anyone to know where I am, especially my father."

The men were astounded at her statements. They listened attentively.

"Sir Boardman, if you would please execute my husband's will for me, I would be obliged. We will need to set up things, so Mr. Cherwin will oversee the mills. You will make sure they are profitable for me, so my children," she patted her stomach again, "will have the means to live in the lifestyle in which my husband left me." She gestured to the mansion they were all in. "Mr. Elmswood, I have a fondness for the horses, and I would appreciate you keeping my husband's stud book thriving and profitable. Keep my father well away from the stables; I don't want him influencing any of my people. I assume, like Mr. Cherwin, that you will hire and fire the necessary people?" The man nodded. "Mr. Adams, can you manage my affairs as you do Miss Lawrence's?"

"No, madam, I cannot; however, that is why I brought Sir Boardman. His knowledge of the law will help sort out this mess, and he can stand up to your husband's solicitors as well as your father. I have plenty on my own plate with Miss Lawrence's properties here in England. I hope you can forgive me?" He looked earnest in his plea to her.

"I certainly understand, Mr. Adams. That was why I contacted you. Thank you for bringing these men here to help me out of this mess," she indicated the sheaves of paperwork again. "If you trust them, then I will trust them as well." She turned to the men. "I may not always agree with you, and I am young, but I hope you will guide me and help me to learn."

"We will, my lady," Sir Boardman promised for them all, and the other two nodded solemnly.

Just then the door opened, and her father waddled in. "There you are. I've been looking–" he left off when he saw the paperwork she had absconded with the other day laying out before strange men he didn't know. "What are you–?" he began, but Abigail arose.

"Father, I'd like to introduce you to my solicitor, Sir Boardman. He will be handling Lord Worthington's will for me. These men will be handling various aspects of the estate as well. I will bid you goodbye as I'm certain you will wish to go home with mother?" she said in a light and cheerful voice.

"He's *what*?" he gasped, as the import of her words sunk in.

"Thank you, Sir Boardman. You may proceed," she said, using the voice she had practiced and was using more often these days. She indicated the will. "Father, I won't be signing your papers. I have been advised not to. Mr. Adams, Mr. Cherwin, and Mr. Elmswood, thank you for your time." They bowed to her, and she added, "I'll speak with you two in the coming days," indicating Mr. Cherwin and Mr. Elswood. She sidestepped her father, who stood with his mouth agape, and she left the room. Going upstairs, she began to pack, knowing that she didn't have a lot of time, and Sir Boardman would be better able to protect her if she got out of this house.

She took several of the ugly gowns she didn't really like, but she knew she would have need of them. She packed her childhood items as well. Two trunks, and she was done. She went to Agatha's rooms next. Seeing the child was not there, she realized she must be being fed at this hour, and she began to pack a third trunk for the child. Ringing for a footman, she had him take the trunk downstairs for her, directing him to come back for her own trunks and arrange for a carriage. It was getting late, and she hurried to find Sir Boardman.

"I'd like you to arrange for people to take me to London and seek accommodations for me," she told him when she found him in her husband's study. "What happened with my father?" she nearly whispered, surprised he hadn't barged in on her while she was packing.

"Your father and mother have left with your sister, brother, and sister-in-law. They were not happy to be sent packing on the day of your husband's funeral; however, I told him in no uncertain terms that he was not welcome here and should leave. Those papers," he pointed to the unsigned documents prepared at her father's insistence, "would have been the end of your freedoms, Lady Worthington. I will be going over your husband's books. I hope you don't mind?" he indicated the stack of ledgers on the desk. "Your father is down, but he isn't out, and those solicitors of your husband's will be filing paperwork to say you were influenced, out of your mind, too young, or whatever they can say to get their hands on this estate." He saw her blanche at that and shook his head. "Do not worry, I won't let them succeed. Is there someone who can travel with you? Someone that can care for you in London?"

"No," she shook her head. "No one I could trust." She thought of Melissa and tried not to let her heart soar. She could write to her and

tell her she was free now. Melissa could come to her, and they could be together at a house where no one knew them. They could be…and then her stomach roiled. She hadn't eaten in hours, and the babe needed nourishment. She couldn't do anything until they knew if this baby was a boy or a girl, and she had to stay hidden until it was born. "It's better that no one know where I am. Can you help me?"

"I will hire a coachman to take you to London. They will go slow to accommodate your condition. I assume little Lady Augusta will be going with you? What about her nurse?"

"I'll need a new nurse. Fire this one, but give her a reference, so she can find another job…just not working for me."

"Any of the other servants?"

"None that weren't loyal to my husband. Mrs. Leister is the housekeeper here. She's a nasty bit of work, but she knows the house very well and runs it with an iron fist. I took these keys from her," she indicated the round set of keys at her waist that she untied and put on the desk. "During my marriage to my husband, she did not give them up."

"You want her fired?"

"No, I really think she would be good for this place, whether I am here or not. Let her do her job, just make sure she knows her place. Mr. Franklin is a good butler. I don't know about the maids or the footmen, none were really anything to me. They were just here, doing the jobs Mrs. Leister wanted them to do. Perhaps we could pare that down?"

He could imagine what it had been like, if what he was gleaning from her existence here was true. He wouldn't ask; he'd wait for her to volunteer the information when she was ready. He had the address of the house in London. It was a good address, and from what the accounts told him, it was minimally staffed. He was writing a letter that she would take with her, so the staff would realize this was indeed Lady Worthington and not some imposter come to take control of the house. He already had her letters of credit in place and would give her them to hand in at the bank. He would go down to London when he had gone over the books and accounts and had ascertained exactly what the Worthington estate entailed. In a few days, he would have detailed lists from both Mr. Cherwin for the mills and Mr. Elmswood for the stables and farms. They'd already been given a list of things to look for. Both were looking forward to the challenges before them and didn't mind working for a woman. Mr. Adams had chosen well. He himself had been surprised to receive the urgent missive from Adams but was pleased because he had become bored with his life, and this would provide him plenty to do in the coming years. He eyed Lady Worthington, wishing he could get to know her better, but his job was to take care of her and her estate. He would do that for her, and he would do it well.

"I will get some men that will be loyal to you and protect you, and they will take you to your new home. We will not let anyone here know where you are going."

"I'm already packed, and the footman is bringing down my trunks."

He was surprised, but he understood her need to get away. Her father wouldn't stop at this. They had caught him unawares, but he would fight back. He had too much to lose and her keeping the knowledge of her pregnancy a secret meant she had power she hadn't even tapped. As the new earl, her son could be managed for many years. He eyed her. Despite her innocent appearance, this young

woman had strength. She probably had to become strong, growing up with Sir Baxter as her father, that weak-willed, bloated…he stopped himself. One man's weaknesses were none of his affair. "There is an inn about an hour's ride in distance. I'll escort you there myself, and you can stay there for a couple of days while I hire men I trust with your care. We can use your carriage, but I'll have men that aren't loyal to your husband handle the horses. You will take those men with you for now, and they can come back here when they are replaced and won't know where you went."

"Let's be on our way soon then. I'll ring for dinner, and then we will go?"

"With pleasure, my lady," he assured her, having forgotten to eat in the hours since their previous repast. He gestured to the door as he escorted her out of her husband's study.

About the Author

K'Anne Meinel is the BEST-SELLING author of LAWYERED, REPRESENTED, SAPPHIC SURFER, DOCTORED, VEIL OF SILENCE, SURVIVORS, VETTED and CAVALCADE as well as several other books including her first, SHIPS which was written in 2003 over the course of two weeks. A gypsy at heart, she has lived in many locations and plans to continue roaming. Videos of several of her books are available on YouTube outlining some of the locations of her books and telling a little bit more…giving the readers insight into her mind as she created these wonderful stories. As of this date she has more than 100 published works including shorts, novellas, and novels. She is an American author born in Milwaukee, Wisconsin and raised in Oconomowoc. Upon early graduation from high school she went to a private college in Milwaukee and then moved to California for seventeen years before returning to the state. Many of her stories have Wisconsin in them as settings for her wonderful, realistic, and detailed backgrounds. Named the lesbian Danielle Steel of her time, K'Anne continues to write interesting stories in a variety of genres in both the lesbian and mainstream fiction categories. Her website is www.kannemeinel.com.

VETTED

If you have enjoyed **OUTBACK YEARNINGS**, I hope you will enjoy
this excerpt from

VETTED

Allyssa is a young college student living her life to please her upper-crust family who want her to take business courses, join her father's business, and marry the "right" man. Allyssa loves animals and yearns to take courses that speak to her heart, but her family are deaf to her pleas and she is unable or unwilling to stand up to them.

Fiona is an older, more established woman; a veterinarian working towards the goal of starting her own large animal practice. When a young woman arrives on her doorstep one night carrying a dog she may have fatally injured with her car, Fiona is thrown for a loop.

Vetted—a life that neither woman anticipated, but each learns they want desperately.

Will their families, the fates, and rustlers finally bring these women to their knees? The only way they can survive is to stand strong together, but are they both ready to fight for what they want? Only time will tell....

Chapter One

Allyssa pushed the gas pedal to the floor of the Volvo station wagon, cursing under her breath as the vehicle slowly responded. Driving her mother's old family 'mobile' was humiliating, uncool, and not at all what she wanted to be driving. She had eyed the sports vehicles for years, but felt a nice Jeep should be in her future. Unfortunately, her funds were limited. Being a student at Colorado State meant she had to take what she could get. This vehicle, not even her mother's station wagon, but the maid's occasional use vehicle, was all she could manage. She was saving her pennies though. She wanted something hip, something cool, and something more in line with her style.

Today, she just wanted to feel the wind whip through her dirty blonde hair and had all the windows down. It was the first time snow wasn't paramount in her mind as the cool spring had turned warm. As she sped past the speed limit, dangerously so, she became more alert and watched for any state troopers hiding in the turnouts or on-ramps; their radar guns aimed at the traffic. Fortunately, this far out on the prairie they were easier to spot, lazier actually, and they rarely came out here unless someone phoned for help from the call boxes on the side of the freeway.

After a while she slowed, took an off-ramp, went up and over the interstate, and onto the on-ramp leading back onto the interstate the other way. She cautiously merged, slowing enough that several faster cars passed her on her left until she was in the slow lane and she began to accelerate. She pushed the gas pedal to the floor again and waited interminably for the old vehicle to respond. She sighed. The speed, the rush of air, and the adrenalin weren't going to do it for her today. She was going to have take what she got, again.

She headed back to the university and her boring dorm room. She had to prepare for her fourth quarter. She'd gotten her midterms from each of the classes. The grades weren't bad, but they weren't stellar and her parents were going to flip. She could already hear her mother, "Allyssa, we expected more of you. Your sister was getting much better grades than this and she managed to be part of a sorority. Why can't you be more like her?" Allyssa knew why she couldn't be more like her sister. She was completely the opposite of her, that's why. Another tactic her mother was sure to throw at her was, "Your father's money isn't really being well-spent, now is it?" The guilt would be heaped on long before her father came home from his day in the office, but his silent condemnation would be worse. He had tried to reason with her mother after the first set of grades came in.

"Now, they said that freshmen frequently falter, and Allyssa is obviously being a typical freshman," but he too would subside under her mother's nervous condemnation of Allyssa's numerous faults.

Allyssa had started to hate going home on weekends. She'd started a job at the cafeteria at school to earn extra pocket change, but as a newbie, she got the less choice hours and weekends, when there were few students to cater to. Those that needed the job more got first choice and she was too new to pick and choose. Her mother had been furious when she found out.

"Are you trying to embarrass us? Your father makes good money and you have an adequate allowance. You don't need to work!"

Allyssa felt compelled to work, to earn her own way. They wouldn't let her do anything she wanted without their opinion, their choices, or their consultation…whether she asked for it or not. Even her choice in career was already mapped out for her.

"Allyssa, you will want to take these business classes if you intend to work for your father when you get out of school. He's made a good living for this family and I'm sure he can get you a job in his office," her mother told her, certain that Allyssa couldn't possibly get a job on her own.

Allyssa didn't want to take business classes. She found them boring and many of her fellow students agreed, some even daring to sleep during the long lectures where some professors preferred to hear themselves speak.

Arriving back at the dorms, she saw it was getting dark and looked for a place to park. She didn't like the way some of the boys were looking at her as she climbed out of the old Volvo. Sure enough, they had to say something to her as she passed by them, looking down at her feet and trying not to be noticed.

"Hey, baby," one of them called.

"You're a tall drink of water, aren't you?" another asked.

Allyssa kept on going, hoping they would stop and leave her alone. She worried that one of them might physically try to stop her. She'd had that experience at a party where they simply wouldn't leave her alone.

"C'mon, baby, a tree like you is meant to be climbed," had been the corny come-on. It had left Allyssa feeling distinctly uncomfortable.

Why anyone would want to be around horny guys all the time she never understood. Still, the silly girls were worse with their giggling and talking about make-up and guys all the time. She shook her head. It was no wonder STDs were so rampant in college-age kids. Half these people were stupid enough to have unprotected sex and then wonder how in the world they contracted something or gotten pregnant. It wasn't just the guys screwing everything in sight, but the girls that were just as bad. The assumption that all girls were like that was what made Allyssa so uncomfortable.

"Whatcha saving it for, baby?" one guy she had dated had the temerity to ask.

It wasn't that she was saving 'it' for anyone. He and his sweaty hands just turned her off.

Even the nice young men at the country club that her mother insisted on introducing her to had some of the same corny come-ons and raging hormones, despite being nicely dressed. Her mother couldn't see it and she tried again and again to introduce Allyssa to her friends' sons, grandsons, and nephews. Many had no desire to date her either, but obligingly went along with their own mother's, grandmother's, or aunt's hopeful intrigue. After all, Allyssa Webster was a catch despite being as tall, if not taller than most of them.

"You have to date a lot of frogs until you find your prince," her father had laughingly warned her as he danced with her at the country club one Friday night. He was one of the few men taller than her and she smiled up at him, wondering how many women he had dated until he found her mother.

Allyssa frequently wondered what was wrong with her that she wasn't interested. She liked the kissing, the cuddling, and the caressing, but when they tried anything more intimate she didn't like the invasion of space or the heated breathing that followed. It reminded her of a panting dog and made her want to laugh.

"Don't worry about her, Helen, our Allyssa is just a late bloomer," her father assured her mother.

"Yes, Allyssa is just our ugly duckling," her mother agreed smilingly, talking as though Allyssa couldn't hear her, couldn't understand, and certainly couldn't make her own decisions.

Tonight, she was feeling restless and the drive had cleared her head for a while, but not long enough. She soon felt the pressures, even unconscious, that her family had put on her broad shoulders. She put out her clothes for the next day, neatly folding her dirty laundry and putting it into a laundry bag to take home the next day for washing. She laid out her books for her classes on Friday and looked once more at the schedule on Monday to be sure she was prepared. She smiled to herself, her mother hadn't noticed when she had dropped Introduction to Business Mathematics and instead took a biology class, something a little more intense than what she had learned back in high school. She hoped her mother would just assume it was something every freshman had to take.

* * * * *

The next day Allyssa went to her classes, plodding along like the masses, looking up as guys her age and even those a little older roughhoused like they were still in grade school. She had been sure she would find more mature people here, after all it was a university, but she was frequently disappointed. The people she was drawn to were more mature, like her professors, who she enjoyed listening to. Their wisdom and knowledge was something she enjoyed. She even attended extra lectures when she could. Anything to avoid the avid drinking and partying that a lot of the freshmen participated in.

As she began to pack up her Volvo for the weekend, two of the girls from her dorm came over to ask her for a ride to the local mall. She knew it was just a way to cop a ride, not to include her in their plans. Still, she was nice enough to give them the ride and was pleasantly surprised when they offered to buy her something at the food court. Looking at the time, she had to decline. Her mother was expecting her for dinner and wouldn't appreciate her being late.

"Can I get a rain check?" she asked carefully and the two of them blinked, not understanding. Sighing inwardly, she asked again, "Another time?"

"Oh yeah, sure," they answered with a smile and turned to go.

Allyssa was sure that people their age should know what a rain check was. She was also sure they had only asked her out of a sense of obligation for the ride, and while a piece of pizza sounded like more fun than her mother's stuffy dinner, she knew she would have had to call first. She really hated her life.

As she pulled up into Regal Crest Gardens where her parents had their home, she closed her eyes momentarily as she saw her sister's car was already parked in her spot. She pulled up in front of the well-manicured lawn and pulled her laundry bag and suitcase from the back seat. Carefully locking the door, she made her way up to the front door only to have her father open it.

"Hey there, Sweet Pea. How was your week?" he asked with open arms to give her a hug. He took her suitcase from her and ushered her into the house.

"It was fine, Daddy. The final quarter starts on Monday," she informed him with a smile as she looked up at him.

"Wow, your first year already finishing up. You didn't think you'd make it, did you?" he teased, knowing she hadn't been thrilled to go to the university. Still, Helen had insisted, and while he didn't agree that everyone needed a college education, he could see her sister had benefited. After all, she had met and married a fine, young man.

"Yep," she agreed, rather than disagree with him as she carried her laundry bag to the laundry room to deposit. The maid would start a load of laundry for her after she got done cleaning up in the kitchen.

Already, she could smell the delicious aromas coming from there. "What's for dinner?" she asked as she came into the kitchen, her father already there. He had deposited her suitcase at the top of the first landing for her and returned to where everyone was congregated around the family room that opened into the kitchen, creating a homey atmosphere.

"It's Friday," her mother said as though that explained it all.

"Can I help?"

"Let your sister do it, dear. She knows how."

Allyssa was used to that response and didn't take offense. Her sister knew all about how to take care of a house—cook, clean and be the good little housewife. She was four years older than Allyssa and seemed to have life well in hand. She and her husband, Derek had a house already as he was well-established in the business he had inherited from his father.

"Hi, Derek. How's tricks?" she teased him as she greeted her brother-in-law.

"Hey there, Beanpole. Where's your beau?" he teased back, never noticing the fleeting hurt look in her blue eyes.

"I can't find one to measure up," she returned, but it was more than what she was saying and no one ever caught it.

"Set the table, dear," her mother ordered her.

Allyssa turned to the small powder room off the family room to wash her hands. Heaven forbid she got germs on her mother's silverware or one of the men in the family set the table.

"You're doing that wrong," Carmen told her as she brought the mashed potatoes to the table, setting it on a heat-absorbing doily so it wouldn't ruin her parents antique dining room set. She quickly reversed the table setting where Allyssa had put the knife on the outside of the spoon instead of the other way around.

"Who cares?" Allyssa mumbled as she finished setting the table. Her mother's Friday evening dinners were monotonous and were only on Fridays because Derek had to work on Sundays. Allyssa would have preferred pizza with someone from school, but who would she have invited?

"Well, you should. What if it were someone important eating with us? The table should be set just so," she indicated as she straightened out an imaginary crease in the tablecloth and then lined up the silverware, glasses, and plates that Allyssa had already put down.

Allyssa didn't argue, Carmen would have come behind her and fixed it anyway if her mother hadn't. Why they bothered to ask her for help she had no idea. She never did it right anyway, at least not to their specifications.

"Go up and change, Allyssa dear," her mother came in carrying the other vegetables, making sure that a cover was on them to hold in the steam.

Allyssa smiled sweetly and did as her mother bid her, changing from her jeans and sweatshirt to a nice dress. She had been tempted to put on a pantsuit, but her mother wouldn't have thought that proper attire and she didn't want to irk her any more than she normally did. Her father would have backed her up and it would have delayed her mother's dinner, ruining it as far as she was concerned. She shrugged into the dress, knowing it wouldn't be up to her mother's standard even though her mother had purchased it for Allyssa.

"Can't you hold your shoulders back and act proud to be wearing that dress?" her mother asked as soon as she saw her daughter. "Stop slouching," she advised, as she brought the main course into the dining room and passed Allyssa.

Allyssa nodded, trying to throw her shoulders back and towering over her mother in the process. She only slouched because her mother always made a big deal about her height. She advised her never to wear her hair up since it made her appear to be even taller.

As they all took their accustomed seats Allyssa wondered what they would do if she sat in a different one. They would probably have minor heart attacks at her temerity. No one would find it funny, and while it might be worth it to see their looks of astonishment or shock, she knew the uproar wouldn't be appreciated by her mother. She expected perfect obedience to her wishes as it was her home and her rules. The rest of them just lived by them.

The talk was first about her father's week and what had happened that might be interesting there. It was the same monotonous job he had had for years and rarely anything different occurred to make it interesting. Allyssa nodded and smiled when expected, eating carefully, one hand on her carefully spread out napkin on her lap, so her mother couldn't find fault. Her sister was watching her like a hawk, quick to find fault if she dared to put her elbow on the table or something equally socially wrong in her eyes.

Next, they discussed Derek's week. His assertions that he was doing well in his business made it sound like boasting. He had increased his father's business by at least thirty percent since he had taken it over right out of college. "They don't do it like that anymore," he had asserted time and again as he modernized things to what he felt they should be doing. Younger meant fresh ideas and more energy in the established business. Some of the old-timers in his father's business had balked at his ideas and plans. One by one they had either quit or retired, preferring not to fight with the original owner's son.

Next, they talked about her mother's week and plans for the next week, which included social engagements since her mother was not allowed to work. Her father insisted she was needed at home to make a happy house for him to come home to. He liked his comforts and he liked how she kept his home for him. He provided Juanita, the maid they had known and employed for the past twenty years, as a sign of his success. She kept the house just the way Helen wanted it.

Next came the conversation about how Carmen was doing. She too was a stay-at-home wife since Derek was doing so well. Occasionally, when they had a rush of orders, she went into work at his business, but for the most part she wasn't using that fine college education they made such a big deal about.

Fortunately for Allyssa, they managed to finish dinner, including a nice meringue dessert her mother had made, before they could start in on her and her week. Hearing about her studies week after week was boring. Nothing changed, and for Allyssa it was hard to come up with anything new and exciting they would want to hear.

"I noticed the Volvo is due for a checkup," her father informed her as they sat in the family room once again and Juanita cleaned up the kitchen and did the dishes. "I'll inform the garage that you'll bring it in next week?"

Allyssa knew she wasn't really being asked as much as informed that it was her 'duty' to keep the old car in good shape. Juanita had been given the new Volvo they purchased to do errands for the family, shop for groceries, and keep their home in order. "Yes, Daddy. I'll do that," she agreed, not wishing to argue.

Allyssa knew that at nineteen they still considered her a kid and treated her as such. Carmen, so much older in many ways, was included in the 'adult' conversation as they discussed current affairs from the newspaper or what they had seen on the television. Children were to be seen and not heard, and Allyssa was relieved when eight came around and Derek announced they better be going.

"I have a golfing date tomorrow if you wish to join us. We tee off at nine," he informed her father who agreed immediately, pleased to be included.

"We could have mimosas at the country club," Carmen told her mother excitedly, including herself in their little outing.

"It's a bit too early for that," Derek admonished and Carmen quickly agreed, subsiding into silence with his greater wisdom.

Allyssa was ready to pull her hair out as she watched her family interact. Why did no one stand up for themselves? Why were they always so polite? If her sister wanted a mimosa at nine in the morning on a Saturday, why couldn't she have one?

"We'll go shopping while they are golfing. Won't that be fun?" Helen asked her daughters, including Allyssa.

"I'd rather..." Allyssa began only to be cut off by Carmen.

"Oh, that sounds great, Mommy. Where will we go?" she enthused.

Without consulting or even really including her in the discussion they mapped out her Saturday. Allyssa knew she would have a headache by noon with their enthusiasm over shopping. She was grateful when Carmen and Derek finished up their plans with her parents and left. She escaped to her room to change out of the uncomfortable dress and pull on a comfortable nightshirt. Sighing deeply, she longed for an escape from this life. She had thought by escaping to live in the dorms, she would have something different. Her life wasn't horrible, but the monotony and sameness of it got on her nerves.

TO BE CONTINUED...

~End sample chapter of BOOK NAME HERE~
For more go to www.Shadoepublishing.com to purchase
the complete book or for many other delightful offerings

~ Because a publisher should stand behind their authors~

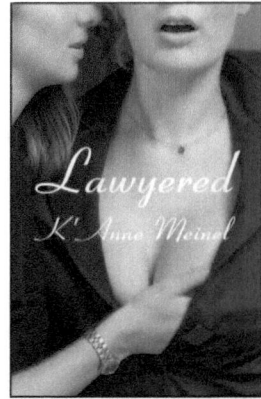
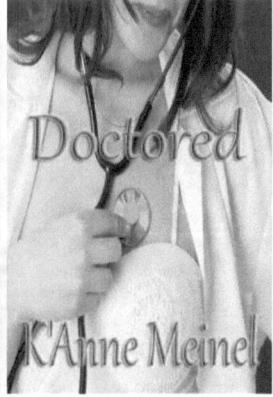

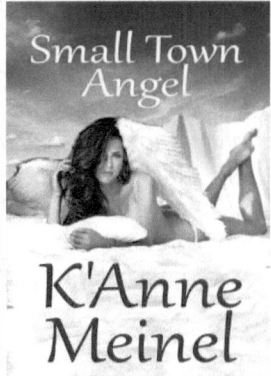

www.shadoepublishing.com

~ Because a publisher should stand behind their authors~

What do you do when you meet someone who changes everything you know about love and passion?

Paige Harlow is a good girl. She's always known where she was going in life: top grades, an ivy league school, a medical degree, regular church attendance, and a happy marriage to a man. Falling in love with her gorgeous roommate and best friend Alyssa Torres is no small crisis. Alyssa is chasing demons of her own, a medical condition that makes her an outcast and a family dysfunctional to the point of disintegration make her a questionable choice for any stable relationship. But Paige's heart is no longer her own. She must now battle the prejudices of her family, friends, and church and come to peace with her new sexuality before she can hope to win the affections of the woman of her dreams. But will love be enough?

www.shadoepublishing.com

When Delaney Delacroix is called to locate a missing girl, she never plans on getting caught up with a human trafficking investigation or with the local witch. Meeting with Raelin Montrose changes her life in so many ways that Delaney isn't sure that this isn't destiny.

Raelin Montrose is a practicing Wiccan, and when the ley lines that run under her home tell her that someone is coming, she can't imagine that she was going to solve a mystery and find the love of her life at the same time.

~ Because a publisher should stand behind their authors~

Carrie flees from the demons of her present, trying to protect the ones she loves.

Frankie hides from the demons of her past, and the memory of loved ones she failed to protect.

A modern day princess thrown to the wolves, Carrie's only hope is the rancher who had spent the better part of a decade in self imposed, near total, isolation. Frankie's history of losing those she tries to save haunts her, but this madman threatens her home, her livestock, her sanctuary. She knows she can't do it alone, has she still got enough support from her oldest friends?

~ Because a publisher should stand behind their authors~

Amelia Gittens had the credit of being the first and only woman thus far in the United States military of being a sniper in combat, made possible by being in the Military Police unit of the crack 10th Mountain Infantry Division. After retirement she joins the City of New York Police Department, and suddenly finds herself involved in a suspect shooting incident which soon encroaches upon her entire life. In order to protect her therapist who has been targeted as a revenge killing, Amelia takes on the responsibility as if she was still in the Army, treating it as a tactical maneuver.

www.shadoepublishing.com

*If you have enjoyed this book and the others listed here
Shadoe Publishing, LLC is always looking for first, second, or
third time authors. Please check out our website @
www.shadoepublishing.com
For information or to contact us @
shadoepublishing@gmail.com.*

*We may be able to help you bring your dreams of becoming a
published author to life.*